Abby Woo

Written by Paul Toritto

31 July 2023

When you love someone . . .

how far will you go?

This book is dedicated to

Barbara Ann Toritto

My beautiful wife who supported

the creation of Abby Woo

And is Abby's biggest fan!

Love you forever and always!

Prologue

Fade to Black

Falling to my knees, my arm dropped limp at my side as my fingers lost grip of the automatic pistol in my right hand. It clattered and spun on the tile floor, empty of its rounds. I had no fight left in me as the light seemed to be fading from the room, growing darker as the sky does after the summer equinox. I crawled to the dead man and took the red and black thumb drive from his coat-pocket; this small object was the solitary reason they had come to the bank today. Mustering the last of my conscious rational ability to think, I stuffed the drive into the thin slot above my jeans pocket, hiding it from anyone who may be looking for it.

Sirens wail from outside the building, and I hear screams from just outside the door of the room I unwillingly occupied. They were painful agonizing calls for help, calling for help to rescue them from the torment of the day. The *pew, pew, pew* from a silenced automatic hand pistol hushed their screams for eternity.

"No witnesses!" were the last spoken words I heard that morning, and the last word I spoke was at a breathless whisper as the room went black . . . *"Abby . . ."*

Earlier that morning . . .

One

Abby Woo

Living in Philadelphia was always a challenge for me because I despised the city and everything it offers. I'm not sure why I stay, other than it's where I grew up and that I have some half ass feeling of loyalty to it. City living offers things like overcrowding, noise, traffic, rundown neighborhoods, crooked politicians, overpriced restaurants, and did I mention traffic? No matter where you went in the city, you went with a crowd. Yesterday I was driving west on Lombard Street, waiting in a long line of traffic to turn right onto South Broad, and the light changed to yellow as I approached the turn, so I stopped the truck. I didn't want to go through the intersection on the yellow, because the department of transportation so harshly enforced the red-light camera laws here. If you were halfway through your turn and the light changed to red, the camera photographed your license plate and police issued you a summons. The city generated vast amounts of income, what they called revenue, from the poor, working slugs like me for one simple reason, right or wrong you always paid the fine. It was more expensive to take a full day off from work to attend traffic court then it was to fork over the hundred and fifty dollars for the ticket and the court costs.

When I came to a stop at the intersection, a sleek red Mercedes AMG sedan hit me from behind. The noise of the vehicles inopportune meeting was the worst part the accident, for me anyway. I exited my vehicle, approached

its rear and surveyed the damaged bumper of my gray-blue
Chevy pick-up truck. It was bent upward a little, but it
didn't make the truck look any worse than it had already. I
scanned the crumpled front end of the sleek red sedan just
as its door opened: a young Asian woman jumped from the
car, animated and irate.

She slammed the car door in frustration and yelled
at me with every four-letter word she could utter, and some
that I never heard before. Guess I would be pissed too; this
Mercedes sedan came with a hefty price tag.

As she approached me, I drifted into a daze. I
flashed her this stupid smile, and I was no longer hearing a
word she said. But, like they sing in those sappy country
music songs, "I knew it from that moment, I was in love."
It's not that lusty fantasy kind of love when you imagine
yourself with a younger woman, it's the spend-the-rest-of-
your-life-with kind of love.

Finally, the yelling stopped, and the young woman
laughed, "Just what the hell are you looking at?"

Snapping from my daydream, I regarded both
vehicles again then looked at the woman. I spoke to her
with my most sarcastic tone. "If you really wanted to meet
me that bad, you should have just said hello. You didn't
have to wreck my truck."

A look of confusion crossed her face as she
remained quiet for a moment. "Wait . . . What! Listen
Mister Piece-of-Shit Pick-up Truck, who's going to pay to
fix my car?"

I thought to myself, "time to make your move Paolo" like I even had a move to make.

"I'll tell you what Miss . . . I'm sorry. What's your name?"

"It's just Abby."

"Tell you what, Abby. Have dinner with me, and I'll pay to fix your car." I waved my hand above the crumpled car. "Even though this was your fault."

Abby put her hands on her hips, mocking my bravado. "So now you're asking me on a date? You wreck my very expensive car with your piece-of-shit truck that's probably not even street legal, and… and… and then you ask me on a date like I'm just waiting for some homeless-looking slob in a crap-ass Chevy to sweep me off my feet. Jesus, what the fuck is wrong with you" Abby had the right to mock me. I was dirty, but after all I had just left work.

"What's wrong with me? Well, nothing out of the norm, and yeah . . ." I hesitated for some dramatic effect. "You wrecked my truck, and now I'm giving you a chance to make it up to me over dinner. Any place you want. My treat. No strings." I raised both hands in pretend surrender as I looked at my truck again.

"Do I look that desperate to you? Do I look like I need you to take pity on me and take me out for a meal? Do you even have insurance on that shit pile? Christ, I can't believe this day!" She retrieved her cell-phone, and dialed a number.

In response to her disbelief, I stepped toward her before speaking again. "What's not to believe? I'm asking for a chance to make this right. Dinner. With me. Your favorite place."

Abby rolled her eyes and turned from me as she told the person on the phone, "I don't know. Hang on a sec." She looked at the car, then at me, and then spoke into her phone again. "I don't know. I'll call you right back." Abby pressed the disconnect icon on her phone as she shook her head in disgust. "How the hell do I know if it's drivable?" she mumbled just loud enough for me to hear.

"It's drivable, just some body damage."

"Can you give it a friggin rest?" Abby leaned against the car door, hung her head and put her hand over her eyes.

I saw she was still steaming mad. "So, what's it gonna be, Abby? Dinner or not?"

She looked at me, and stuttered a bit when she spoke and laughed at the same time, "God, I don't even know your name. And why the hell would I want to go out with you? You can't even make a right turn onto another street."

After a breath she continued, "How the hell can you get to the restaurant without killing yourself?"

Now it was my turn to laugh, "Well." I began as charmingly as I could. "My names Paolo, and, as far as getting there alive, well, all the more reason for you to go and find out?" Time seemed to slow to a crawl, like in those movies when something big would happen.

Abby puckered her lips as her right foot tapped to some unheard musical beat, all the while in thought and trying not to allow the smirk on her face to spread to a smile. She looked at me, stepped forward, then poked me in the chest with her right forefinger. "You know what? It's a date! And I hope you have something nice to wear, like maybe some homeless-guy dress suit or something. This'll cost you big time, Mister. You can take me to Vetri's on Spruce Street. Make the reservation for eight on Friday night, and don't forget your wallet. It's the best damn Italian restaurant on the east coast" Then she thought for a moment more. "On second thought, I'll meet you there. And don't be late. I hate when people are late."

I was willing to play her game of give-and-take bantering. "What? You won't let me drive you there?"

"Not On Your Life . . . or in this case, my life. Don't forget to make reservations. You really don't want to see me disappointed."

I smiled as she approached the police officer rolling down his patrol car's window. She summarized what happened, told him everything was handled, and that we did not need his help. He looked at me. I shrugged in response to his unspoken question. He rolled up the window and drove off. One thing was left to do now as far as dinner with Abby. I yelled after her as she called someone again. "Excuse me. Abby! You didn't give me your cell number." I walked toward her.

She looked at me as I heard her describe her cars damage. "NO, the jackass who caused the accident said it's drivable. I'll bring it straight over. See you in a few." Abby disconnected and slid the phone into her rear pocket.

As I stood next to her, she took my cell phone from my hand and entered her number. After she drove off, I look at the name she saved into my contacts list. A grin crossed my face as I read, "*LearnToDriveJackass*" on the screen.

I don't know much about dating. It was one area in which I thought of myself as a complete amateur. I waited until Wednesday afternoon to call Abby. I didn't want to seem overanxious about seeing her again. I was hoping it appeared that I was playing it cool. I wanted to let her know I had made reservations, as she had suggested, give her the details about the planned night out, and to hear her voice again.

She answered on the third ring without a hello, "What the hell took you so long to call? I thought I would have to hunt you down to pay for my Benz."

I didn't know what to say. I was a bit stunned and stammering for a response.

"Hello . . .? she asked mockingly. Is there anyone on the other end of this conversation? Hello!"

God was she a ball buster! I finally found my voice, "Hey, Abby. It's Paolo DeLuca. I just wanted to confirm with you for Friday night. I made reservations for eight, like you asked. I hope you still plan on coming with me."

And as soon as the words were out, I thought it sounded pathetic.

"Feeling a bit inadequate Paolo?" I heard a laugh in her voice. "And I'm not coming with you, remember, I'm meeting you there. I would like to get to the restaurant in one piece, so I can enjoy a great meal, completely at your expense. By the way, how much did you have to pay to bribe Riccardo for a table on a Friday night?"

I chortled. "I paid less for my truck."

I heard a real laugh from her this time. "Well, I've seen your truck, Paolo, and if you're trying to impress me, you're going to have to try harder." I could tell she was stifling another laugh. "I'll have to talk to Riccardo Friday night. He let you off cheap. I'll see you there."

Just like that, I stood with the phone still to my ear, as if she had put me on hold. "Real smooth jackass," I said to myself.

Finally, Friday came, but the day dragged. I thought eight o'clock would never arrive. I was a bit nervous, and I haven't had this many butterflies since my grade-school performance in *Peter Pan.* To avoid further embarrassment, I parked the truck two blocks from the restaurant. I walked south, crossed the street, in-between some double-parked vehicles and entered the building as the maître-d opened the door for me with a polite, "Good evening Mr. DeLuca."

A European woman was waiting for me just inside, standing proudly with her hands clasped in front of her.

"Good evening Mr. DeLuca. Please follow me." She said with a smile.

She didn't need to see if my name was in the reservations book resting on the lectern's top. Someone must be well known here, and I'm sure it was Abby. "Please wait here Mr. DeLuca, and please enjoy your evening." I smiled a *thank you* and nervously checked my watch. 7.55 p.m.

A well-groomed Italian man approached me, "You must be Miss Woo's eight o'clock. Follow me please." He led me to the chef's table as visions of dollar signs danced in my head. "From Miss Woo, sir. She said to tell you that she'll be a few moments late, and she also asked that I tell you to enjoy the wine and not to wait for her to open the envelope."

I took a sip of wine and place the tall stemmed crystal goblet on the white linen tablecloth. "What's this?" I asked, as if someone just gave me a note to take home to my mother.

Riccardo laughed politely, "Knowing Miss Woo, I would expect it's the bill for the repairs to her Benz."

I turned about the same shade of red as the wine. "Jesus, does everyone in town know about the accident?" I gulped down the rest of the wine and asked for a second glass before peeking inside the envelope. When I saw the total on the bill, my heart stopped for a moment. This night was costing me big time, and Abby wasn't even here yet.

Twenty minutes later, Abby finally arrived. The staff greeted her with warm hugs and kisses on each cheek, like they were family. Riccardo greeted her with a kiss on the hand and a smile that said *welcome home.* He showed her to the table as I stood to greet her and help her with her chair.

Again, I was amazed at how naturally beautiful she was. Abby wore a short gray sweater dress over black leggings, the complementing black belt was several inches wide and fastened with a silver chain and buckle. Knee high leather boots with silver ornamental chains completed her ensemble. I tried to speak after she was seated, but all that escaped was a squeak. Abby knew she pulled off this look, and she did it very well, she radiated self-confidence, I gained control of myself and took a gulp of wine.

"Hello Paolo. Do you like the wine?"

I stammered, "Best I've ever had."

Abby raised her hand, and the waiter approached with menus. "No thank you Timothy." She smiled at me. "Paolo, will you trust me?"

I shrugged, "Of course."

"Timothy, please bring us two of my usual."

"Very good Miss Woo." He turned to go place our order.

I watched him disappear into the kitchen area, "So, what did we just order?"

Abby smiled, "Don't worry. You'll love it. Oh, I see you got my envelope. Just pay it directly, no need to get me in the middle. More wine?"

Abby and I shared a wonderful meal with elegant wine and great conversation. I had never talked so long about so much with anyone. We finished the night with espresso and the best cheesecake on Earth.

"Told you this was the best Italian on the east coast," Abby said matter-of-factly.

I gave Timothy my Visa card and asked Abby what she had planned for the rest of the night.

"PJ's, more wine, and curling up with a good book. How about you?"

"I think I'll go back to the garage and pull some overtime to help pay for this date."

Abby smiled at my attempt at a joke.

The waiter returned with the check, I added the twenty percent for the tip and signed the receipt without thinking anymore about the total as Abby asked Timothy to have her car brought around. I escorted her to the valet station where her car was already waiting. The valet held the door for her as she handed him a twenty.

He thanked her and the said, "Good evening, Miss Woo."

She turned to me with a soft smile, "Thanks for a great dinner. I had more fun than I thought I would, or expected. Good night, Paolo."

Abby kissed me on the cheek, got into her car, and drove off. Leaving me standing there with my finger-tips on my cheek, like I was a schoolboy after his first crush had kissed him. As she left the restaurant's driveway, she beeped the horn twice.

I was a bit embarrassed when the valet asked me to move to the sidewalk. It clicked a moment later, Abby's car had been repaired and had been returned to her.

"Damn, she is one resourceful woman."

"You got off easy Mac," the valet said.

I looked at him with a puzzled expression. I guess he knew about the accident too.

After that night at the restaurant, Abby and I were together as much as possible. It just seemed so natural for me to be with her. How often do you hear people say something about finding their soulmate? I know Abby is mine. We had some great times together, but one day stands out as what I would say was our real first date.

We explored an abandoned medical facility in another part of the state on a warm Saturday afternoon. Gaining access to the property through a well-used break in the chain link fence, we roamed in and out of several buildings on the property, holding hands and standing as close together as possible. Things progressed from there, and we became intimate after finding a secluded place. Afterwards, Abby made me promise one thing, that no matter the situation, I would always call her *Abby*, never by her full first name, Abhijishya. Even if we were to argue, or if I was angry with her, she made me promise it would always be *Abby*. Since I had never seen her so serious about any subject, I agreed. Immediately, she returned to her normal self with no signs of worry.

Abby wanted to be called *Abby* for reasons of a deep personal and at times debilitating nature. She was unable to trace her ancestry beyond herself, and she felt it left a hole inside her that nothing could fill. She also said that using her full name gave her a feeling of partial emptiness, like she was only part of what she should be.

"You mean like spiritually" I asked, hoping to give her a direction to look in.

"No, it's more than that."

Abby was the definition of an independent woman, but this one thing made her desperate to find something, anything, and even anyone to help her know where she came from. She wanted to know who her birth parents were, she wanted to know why they gave her up for adoption, or, in her words, "gave her away." She knew her cultural background was Chinese, but she wanted more information on her bloodline. None of this mattered to me, I loved Abby for who she was, but, to her, it was all important.

I did the I'm-the-man-thing many times; I insisted I pay for our evenings out. Abby didn't think it was necessary, but it was one of the few things I remember my father ever talking to me about. He told me, "Always treat a woman like a lady, that way she'll respect you as a man." I tried to live up to that, because my dad never really spoke about anything at all. To my memory, he had never said, "I love you," or anything else Italian family members say to each other. I'm sure it was one of the thousand reasons I left home at seventeen, never to return again, not even for the funeral. Bad blood is bad blood.

Sometimes Abby would have a few drinks, let her defenses down, and lose control of the rope that held up the curtain which hid her vulnerabilities. That's when the need to find her past overtook everything else. On occasion, it was so bad that we argued about it, but most of the time I played the supportive male role without missing a beat and encouraged her to find out who she "really was."

Abby had even gone the route of hiring several private-detectives who had done nothing more take her money and feed her bullshit. Three different PI's and almost ten thousand dollars later, she was no closer to discovering anything about anything. I had met the last investigator she had hired, he looked as if he fit the Magnum PI role, but, if I were to grade his skills, "sucked" would be the appropriate word to put on the tell-us-what-you-think survey card. After I read him the riot act about money on Abby's behalf, of course, without her knowing, he gave her what little he could find. This too, along with other bits and pieces of hope, would end up in a safety deposit box at Franklin Bank and Trust.

I slept over one Friday night, and, the next morning I made us breakfast. When she finished eating, she went to do some gardening, this helped her meditate and calm her nerves. Abby's backyard was beautifully decorated in the spirit of an Asian garden, it was almost as beautiful as its owner. I watched her for a bit. Beholding the beauty of the garden and the gardener gave me unlimited joy.

Sitting within the confines of this vine-covered veranda, I sipped black coffee and relinquished my gaze on Abby and her garden to return to reading the morning paper, which is a bit of an outdated activity, but reading the paper is a way to hold onto days gone by. They were not the best days; however, some were unforgettable, and some I pushed to the bottom of my soul to hide them from the light of day. They needed to remain locked away, like all family secrets, kept in a cedar chest in the attic never to be seen again by any family member.

Today's headline was just another in a long line of dramatics influenced by the Philadelphia Morning Bulletin editors. Someone had bested them with the story of the revitalization of Franklin Park tract, which borders on Abby's backyard. In turn, they overexposed, and over-exaggerated any issue related to the project, which they used as fodder for a theatrical headline. Today it read, *"Second Lead Contractor Found Hanged on Parks Opening Day."*

"Contracting is a rough business these days," I thought. Flipping the paper to read below the fold, I took another sip of bitter coffee, but I again was drawn to gaze at Abby and her garden. I was in awe of its beauty, but I was stunned by the beauty of the gardener as she worked in the flower beds. As if my love extended and touched her shoulder, she glanced at me for a moment, and, within that moment, a smile appeared, expressing her love in return. Our connection to each other had become so much more

than physical, it was almost as if it was spiritual, as if a higher power had preordained our meeting and our lives together.

Looking past Abby toward the trees that border the park and distinguish the property line of the backyard, I saw dark shades of brown, which, in turn, were highlighted by a rainbow of green hues. This was a drastic change compared to what Abby had told me how the yard appeared just last year. Franklin Park took three years of on again, off again construction and fierce court battles to complete, but; the final result was well worth it.

According to today's article, Franklin Park was the largest undertaking in the history of Lauren Paul Creations, the designer, developer, and contractor for the park. Lauren Paul was obviously a professional moniker; the name did not fit his noticeably Asian heritage. The paper said he was as flamboyant as he was bold with his eleventh-hour redesign of the park. He took the original ideas of Worldwide Concepts, the first contractor, and after an additional six-million dollars, gave birth to what some called the eighth wonder of the world. Worldwide Concepts pulled out of the project after the police discovered the company's founder and owner dead in the park during the early stages of its development. His hands had been removed at the wrists, leaving many to speculate about possible ties to the criminal element that inhabited the city. It was a statement to others interested in entering their opinions of the parks design, "Hands Off." The company dissolved quickly after its owner's death, and none of its employees ever spoke of its downfall, nor would they, even when threatened with imprisonment.

Franklin Park's landscaping was amazing in its beauty. The flowers Abby had planted along the fence line complimented the park's landscape, and they also attracted the rarest of wildlife. One of the vine-like plants interwove itself through the steel wire fence, and, when it bloomed, its flowers were funnel shaped with yellow petals trimmed with a thin black edge. That edge made the flowers appear to be wearing eye-liner. And it's why they were called yellow eye shadows. In turn the fragrance of the eye shadows attracted a miniature species of bird whose wings fluttered so quickly they seemed to become invisible. The creature appeared to float motionless as it sucked the flowers nectar to sustain its life.

"So beautiful!" I thought as I watched Abby observe the birds, Spring is Abby's favorite time of year. She said it was because life is renewed and new beginnings are possible, I have to agree with her, Abby and I were a new beginning, full of new possibilities. My life with her will be amazing.

Abhijishya, (pronounced a-bee-JEESH-ya, whose name translates to "Independent Girl") was a twenty-four-year-old medical student, who performs on occasion with the Philadelphia Philharmonic Orchestra as a guest violinist. A childless couple who had lavished her with all the educational opportunities available to people with money had adopted her. Because of how brilliant she was, a 135 IQ, her stepparents wanted her to follow them into the medical field, but her first love had always been classical music. Abby had quit medicine one-year shy of completing her residency to follow her dream of playing in a professional orchestra. Her discussion to chase her dream had probably been my doing, as was the recent tattoo now gracing her lower back. Those were two of the many reasons I thought her adoptive parents hated me; however, Abby was a brilliant violinist, and the music came natural to her. She once told me that she could see the music as she played the notes. I guess I could call her a prodigy, but she is just so damn good at playing. How could she not share this gift with the world around her, no matter what her parents thought. So, I bared the cross of their anger over her career change. It's better that they hate me than Abby. She was already looking for so much from her past, I'd hate to have her looking to reconnect with her adoptive parents on top of all her other troubles.

Abby also mentioned possibly attending Julliard. She thought about it at the constant urging of the orchestra's lead conductor. He had contacts at the school and could guarantee an invitation to attend. He had sent an audition video to the school's admissions board, without Abby's knowledge, in hopes she would attend to refine her skills. Graduating from Julliard would ensure a spot as first violinist with the Philadelphia Philharmonic Orchestra. She told her stepfather, and he was off-the-handle upset, demanding she return to work to complete her medical training, and to forget her silly ideas of being a violinist. I disagreed with him, and I told him as much, hence the rift between both Dr. Rubins, Abby, and I.

I had my reason for standing firm and agreeing that Abby should move on. The first time I saw her play with the orchestra, I was mesmerized. The house lights dimmed as the stage up-lights came to life, adding a soft glow to Abby's natural beauty. I remembered watching her walk across the stage in her favorite Vera Wang gown, her waist-length black silk hair flowed gracefully on the air until she found her mark. She was a vision of beauty that night, as always. Sitting in the seats reserved for family, I watched Abby prepare for her violin solo. She looked toward me and noticed that her parent's seats were vacant, and frowned for only a moment. She performed the solo barefooted, she told me afterward it was so she could feel the vibration of the music's rhythm vibrate through the stage floorboards as the orchestra played. Her performance was met with a standing ovation in response to its inspiring beauty. This is what Abby was meant to do, share her love of music with all who would listen, and to share her love with me, something I was so grateful for.

Returning to reality, I decided to get on with the day. I folded the paper, swiveled from the patio chair. I headed into the kitchen and put everything into the dishwasher, wiped down the counter, and placed the paper in the recycle caddy under the sink.

When Abby came in from gardening, I told her I would go to the bank with her today. I wanted to make up for last night's argument about, what else, Abby looking for Abby and her drastic mood change. I knew she was pissed at me for what I had said last night, but she had never been this cold and distant before. I chalked it all up to her late-night orchestra performance, the last bottle of her favorite cheap wine, Yellow Tail, and long hours of internet searches, which concluded with me sleeping on the couch again. The only difference was this time she woke me up when she finished her web-surfing for the night. She shoved me out of bed and yelled, "Go sleep on the fucking couch!" So, I did. I apologized, because, one: I was wrong to be so hard on her, and two: because my frigging back hurt from sleeping in such an awkward position on the most uncomfortable couch in existence.

I insisted on taking the Chevy for the bank errand, I thought it made sense, since it needed a fill-up, you know, the two-birds-with-one-stone thing.

On the way, Abby laid into me again, "Seriously Paolo! How much longer do you expect me to ride around in this piece of shit? When will you break down and get something a few years newer? Christ, what if someone I know sees me in this thing? It's really fucking embarrassing."

I took a sideways glance at Abby and was a bit confused about her outburst. "We had this conversation last week, babe. Don't you remember? I told you that I love this truck and that's when you laughed at me for being so emotionally attached to it. 'We've been through a lot together,' you apologized for forgetting it was my dad's truck."

Abby looked unsure, but the look on her face disappeared as quickly as it had appeared. It was almost as if she thought we had never had this conversation. "Drop me here, and I'll walk the rest of the way. I don't want anyone in the bank seeing me get out of this thing."

I pulled over, and Abby jumped out while telling me she'd meet me inside. Some passerby mocked me as I dropped the truck into gear and started to pull away, "Hey buddy, the junk yard is two blocks up!" I shook my head as I thought, "Only in Philly!"

I parked the truck one block over, in the first available spot, and paid at the parking kiosk. I met Abby in the bank just as the manager was greeting her. "Nice to see you again Miss Woo, how are you today?" The woman tried to engage Abby in conversation as if they were more than acquaintances, resulting in Abby looking irritated, impatient, and speaking rudely to the woman. Since I had met her, I have never seen her act like this toward anyone. She was always cordial, except for today. I'm not sure what it was, but Abby seemed out of place somehow. I shook it off and figured it was part of her obsession with finding her birth parents. Today was probably one of those bad days, and Abby's tone was a result of a late-night performance, too much wine, too many hours on the web, and too little sleep.

Abby hoped this ritual of adding bits and pieces of information to her collection, which she had all cataloged and kept compulsively organized in a safety deposit box at Franklin Bank and Trust, would give her answer to the one lingering mystery in her life which consumed her. She had organized every piece of paper and every trinket in the deposit box with perfection only a person with deep OCD could master. She prayed it would lead her to an answer one day, but now, she may never find any answer to where her roots lie.

Today's visit to the bank was supposed to be to add another critical piece of evidence of who Abby may be to the small but growing pile inside the deposit box. The vault itself was huge, holding almost one-thousand boxes for customers to keep their valuables safe from the lowlifes of the city, and boasting ample storage for an untold amount of cash. The area just outside the main vault offered eight rooms, four on each side, with red velvet curtains that could be drawn for privacy. The room reminded me of something seen in spy thriller movies where the hero with no memory of his past found passports, money, and guns to offer a clue as to who he was. A bit of déjà vu, if you ask me.

The branch manager helped retrieve Abby's box from its resting place in the blue-gray steel wall, placed it on the table in front of her, and, with a last gesture, she unlocked one of the two locks necessary to gain access to its contents. This was an added measure of security Franklin Bank offered, and then she left us alone to go through its contents. Abby stared at the box, as if not sure what to do next.

I asked her if she was okay, she replied, "Fine, just a bit tired, that's all." And unlocked the second lock, flipped open the lid and reached inside. I was thinking something was off, her answers didn't seem quite right to me. Something was nagging at the back of my brain, but maybe we were both, "Just tired." It had been one of those weeks followed by one of those nights.

The first thing retrieved from the box, as always, was her necklace. She held it in her hand, admiring its splendor a bit longer than normal, and then put it around her neck. The necklace was the only real material link to her past. She had it from childhood, somehow past down from her birth mother, and kept it here at the bank like it was something from an ancient time and something she wanted to be sure didn't get misplaced. It was beautiful, even to me, a guy with no eye for material possessions. The necklace was a huge inverted tear-drop-shaped deep blue stone set inside a gold dragon-shaped diamond pendant setting with a twenty-four-inch gold rope chain. Inside the bank was the only place Abby ever wore the necklace. She said she kept it here not because of its monetary worth, but because of its sentimental value. It's something that can't be replaced, and she would be devastated if it were lost.

I remember the first time I saw the necklace; I was speechless. It caught a sliver of light as Abby held it in her hand, causing it to sparkle like fireworks on the Fourth of July, a breathtaking rainbow of colors. That was the first time she had told me its story. I composed myself and asked her if she knew its value. She glared at me across the table with anger in her eyes; an anger I had never seen before. The way I asked must have sounded like I was only concerned about its monetary value, so I backed off a bit and rephrased the question. "Abby, is this worth anything other than the sentimental value you have for it?"

Abby took a few quiet moments to breathe deeply, calming herself, and expelling the anger. "Sorry, I asked the bank manager to have it appraised for me. It really was her recommendation after she had seen me wearing it. Insurance reasons she suggested. She had this guy come in from Rosenburg's Diamond Exchange as a favor. Anyway, I told him it was a one-of-a-kind family heirloom, which is why I love it so much, and he was surprised by the necklace and asked me if I knew what I had here. I told him it had belonged to my birth mother."

"And?"

"Well, first he asked me if I wanted to sell it to him, and, of course, I said no."

"Come on Abby, stop stalling. How much did he tell you it was worth?"

"He said about four and a half million."

I opened my mouth to speak but nothing came out.

Abby put her hand under my chin and pushed it shut. She gave me that coy smile that I love so much, the one that said, "I'm happy," and the one that appeared when she knew she had gotten the best of me.

I tried to speak again, but the only thing that came out was, "Holy shit!"

I had just stopped the memory when the day erupted into chaos. It may have been a coincidence of a random chance that we were in the rear of the bank and within the anti-chamber of the vault when the robbery began. Abby and I were two of the few people left alive, but still affected by the initial destruction from the explosions. We, along with the bank's manager, had survived by being in the right place at the wrong time. We were lucky enough to have the anti-chamber walls leading into the vault shield us as the explosions happened.

Two

Caught in the Act

The room spun and my ears rang from the blast. Everything sounded hollow and muffled as it all echoed off the sound-deadening walls. Abby shook me hard, pushing back and forth on my shoulder to rouse me from my stupor as I lie on the tiled floor. With my eyes half open and the scene around me blurred, the only thing in focus was Abby's face.

Dust and debris from the blast settled on her cheeks as tears streaked toward her chin. She continued her attempts to bring me around and pushed harder while calling my name over and over, with a *"please wake up"* thrown in here and there.

I wasn't sure what the hell had just happened, but realization finally settled in. Automatic gun fire erupted just outside the anteroom's door, and I heard screams from what I now know were the murders of the tellers and customers left alive after the grenade explosions. I pulled Abby close to me. I took her chin in my left hand shushed her with a finger to my lips as if I were scolding a schoolgirl for being too loud in class. Leaning in close so I was just an inch from her ear, I whispered loud enough so just Abby could hear me. Goosebumps formed on her skin as my lips found her earlobe, "Stay with me. Breath normally, but above all else, don't make a sound."

As I stood, I hoisted Abby up with me while scanning the area for someplace to hide. We approached the other side of the anteroom where the upturned desk, which had served as a place for people to sit and view their valuables, now offered a possible safe harbor. I pushed Abby down between the wall and the desk and covered her with my body as best I could. This offered nothing more than a momentary asylum from the unknown madness outside the vault room.

I tried to keep Abby calm, but she would not stop whimpering, no matter what I said to her. In a last-ditch effort to quiet her, I pinched her forearm as hard as I could. It got her attention. Her head snapped toward me with anger in her eyes, but the action had its desired effect. Abby had stopped crying and was quiet and alert while rhythmically rubbing the sting from her arm.

The door to the anteroom had blown almost shut from the blast, and someone was yanking it open on its last remaining hinge. The steel door squealed in agony as two men in loose-fitting black clothing ran through it and past our hiding spot. They entered the vault at a rapid purposeful pace and never noticed us. Their oversized clothing hid their shapes as the black pull-over wool winter hats masked their identities from any remaining surveillance cameras, and also from me and Abby. Each of the silhouetted performers held automatic weapons. I recognized several weapons, one man brandished a Nikonov light machine gun, and the other wielded a Makarov semi-automatic pistol. The pistol normally holds a fifteen-round magazine, and anyone that used one always had one in the chamber.

The second robber into the room manhandled the bank manager, forcing her into the vault. He had a fist full of her short-cropped hair, pulling her in the direction he wanted to go. She winced in pain, but her expression was one of fear. She muttered something unintelligible while she cried out in whimpers of fright. The only reason she could still be alive was because of the optical scanner, which allowed access to the deepest reaches of the vault, the place where Abby's bank box had once resided.

This bank was state of the art with all kinds of gadgets to deter crime, too bad they proved useless. The optic scanner with its retina mapping and the blue-hued light on the palm reader with pulse detection, was supposed to make it impossible to burglarize the bank's vault. You needed to be breathing and have a pulse to gain access to the vault and its treasures.

Again, I put my finger to my lips as a signal for Abby to remain quiet. She nodded in understanding with tears still in her eyes and a tight grip on my arm.

I peeked up over the desk and saw the backs of three people facing the room that held the deposit boxes. My assessment was these guys had to be connected to something or someone, because their kind of firepower was something one couldn't possibly buy for just a few hundred dollars from a street thug, especially Russian made gear. The taller man slung his weapon over his back and grabbed the bank manager's right hand. He placed her palm on the scanner and, with a fist full of hair, shoved her head toward the retinal scanner. Both actions needed to be done simultaneously to gain access to the caged room.

A soft musical tone sounded just after the scans had completed, and a computer-generated voice came over an unseen speaker. "Identity confirmed. Access granted. Good morning, Miss Stone, I hope you are having a pleasant day."

"Small chance of that," I thought as I watched the encounter transpire.

"What's happening?" Abby asked.

I ducked down and told her what I had just seen. "Stay down. Get ready to move." I peeked over the desk again then whispered in Abby's ear. "When I say move, get your ass out the door, and don't look back. Do you understand?"

"But what about_"

"No buts, Abby. I'll distract them, and when I say move, you goddamn move! Now, tell me you understand."

"Okay, okay! Now what about you?"

I signaled for her to be quiet again, then I returned to peering over the desk.

Another predator stood just outside the damaged steel door counting down in ten-second intervals and then marking them with such phrases such as, "Ninety seconds!"

The taller man roughhoused the bank manager deep inside the vault, probably to open whatever boxes she could. She protested and the thief grabbed her hair again, and, with all his strength, slammed her face into the wall of the steel gray containers, a stream of blood started flowing from her nose and mouth.

She wiped her mouth with the back of her hand, "Please, I . . . can't."

With each of her protests, the tall man grabbed her hair and yanked it until she screamed. This time, she was on her toes as he pulled her from the floor, then, he let her go, and she'd fall to the floor again.

"I can't do this," she slurred through the sobs and tears.

He grabbed a hand full of hair and pulled her entire body backward with all his strength. With a loud grunt, he flung her body forward and slammed the top of her head into the wall. She slid down the wall in slow motion, unconscious, bleeding from a cut in her forehead.

"Christ Mike! Take it easy. We can't get what we came for without her."

"No names, asshole! Shut the hell up and give me the count."

"Sixty seconds, jackass. If we don't get what we came for, you know what she'll do."

"Yeah! Fuck her too! This bitch is making me crazy."

The man pulled her up again as she regained consciousness. Every time the woman protested; the tall man would slam her into the wall of boxes.

"Listen to me . . . please," she pleaded, unable to stand on her own. "I . . . can't open the box! I couldn't get the swipe key. I think they might suspect something."

"Shut the fuck up bitch! Once more, just once more and I'll kill your fucking family. I swear to God I'll kill your family. I'll get Max on the phone, and_" his voice became almost too soft to hear. "I'll tell him to kill the little one first, and I'll make you watch it on the video link while he cuts the little bastard's throat. Now, do your fucking part like you agreed."

I ducked back down behind the desk, "Shit. She's in on it."

"No way." Abby said as if she knew the woman well enough.

This building housed the main branch of Franklin Bank, which boasted an ultra-modern thirty story high rise on Fifth and Market Streets, and it was the newest of the bank's multimillion-dollar facility and also its corporate headquarters. Just to the right of the large gold embossed logo, hung a pictorial history of all of the management personnel the Franklin Bank had employed since its founding. The woman the thug was slamming around was the first female to rise to the level of branch manager in the corporation's history. Emma Stone, a third generation German American, was just twenty-eight and the youngest person to ever reach her position at the bank. She exhibited the type-A personality that led someone to success at whatever endeavor they set their sights on. Miss Stone, a single mother of two, was destined to be a superstar in the world of banking, until today happened. This group of somehow connected gangsters held her family captive to ensure her participation in today's events.

Knowing some history of any hostage situation, Miss Stone's family was probably already dead, they just hadn't told her. I'm sure they died just after she and the bank crew left her house earlier this morning. Their deaths would ensure no loose ends remained, along with no one to identify the thieves. My initial thoughts were, that the manager was helping to rob her own bank, but it was much more than that.

The manager finally pulled a box from its resting place in the wall and placed it on the closest flat surface. She begged again for her life and the life of her children.

The tall man hit her with the butt of his pistol on the side of her head, again drawing blood from her pale skin. "Jesus, just open the fucking box!" He pushed the barrel of the gun into her temple.

As the gun forced her head sideways, she pulled an electronic keycard from her blazer pocket. She must have requested a duplicate from corporate on one of the upper floors. She must have lied to corporate to get another key, a customer's key, and had just lied again to the man in black that she wasn't able to get it. Deception resided in every word she spoke now. It was obvious to me that she was conflicted in her role as mother and in her role as manager, but, in the end, no one would blame her. She was just trying to save her family, as any mother would.

With both keys in their slots, the crew leader slammed open the box lid and removed a single SanDisk flash drive, admiring it and raising it victoriously.

"We're outta time," the other man said. "Gotta move! Now!"

The tall man clicked something on his belt, "Item secured." He tossed the drive to his partner who placed it in his jacket pocket.

In one final attempt, the manager pleaded, "Let me go. Let me go to my family, please . . ."

The tall man put the pistol to Stone's forehead. "Why can't you just shut the fuck up, you lying bitch?"

A single shot splattered her brains on the wall behind her.

Abby screamed and gave away our hiding spot.

The men pulled us from our safe haven.

Abby cried franticly as I held her tight to me.

The shorter man looked at us and then at the tall man. He pointed his Makarov at both of us.

I stepped in front of Abby and begged him not to shoot. "No one else has to die. We'll do whatever you want. Just go, and we'll never say a word."

The tall man grabbed Abby and pulled her from behind me. He started to say something but he spotted her necklace. His eyes lit up like he had just won the lottery.

He spoke to his partner in another language, and the other one looked at Abby. She knew instantly,

"You're not taking the necklace. It's mine, you fucking assholes."

The tall man ripped off his mask and hit her face with the pistol.

Abby crumpled to the floor with a bleeding lip.

The other guy hit me with the butt of his weapon. I almost blacked out but managed to stay alert.

From outside the room, another man yelled, "Police are here! Let's move!"

The tall man pulled at Abby's necklace, but she grabbed his arm and refused to let it go as they struggled.

"Abby, let him have it. It's not worth your life!"

He hit her again, and again, until she let go of the jewel.

I jumped at the shorter gunmen.

He managed to hit me with the weapon again, and I stumbled backwards. Managing to get my footing, I launched myself once more at the shorter thug, punching him in the face with all the force I had left in me.

He fell to the carpeted floor unconscious as I grabbed his pistol.

The guy outside the vault yelled again, "We gotta fucking move. Now!"

The tall man had Abby in a choke hold while dragging her backwards toward the exit and using her as cover.

I aimed the pistol at his head but was too disoriented to fire accurately. When I pulled the trigger, the shot went wide, and the round bounced off the vault's door with a loud ping. I raised the pistol again, and just as I squeezed the trigger, I felt a sharp thump in my gut. I felt the slug hit me before I heard the shot.

Abby screamed.

The crew yelled, "Get out now! Police all around! Bring that useless fucking bitch with us," and then more gunfire.

I was on the edge of blackness. All I could hear was Abby screaming, "Nnnooooo! Let go of meeee!"

Then in reply, "We'll need her to get out of here. Let's move!"

I fell to my knees, wondering if this was some kind of nightmare. I faded in and out of consciousness as the gun tumbled from my hand. I couldn't help Abby. I reached for her, "Abby . . . I . . . love . . ."

Things were confused with all the commotion and the arrival of the police SWAT units. Time was moving too fast for the thieves to think rationally. In their haste to escape the bank with Abby in tow, the tall man never went to his downed comrade, the man who had put the flash drive in his pocket.

I managed to crawl to his partner and take the drive from his pocket. I pushed it deep into the small slit above the pocket on the front of my jeans. The world went black.

My last memories were seeing the tall man dragging Abby from the vault as the bank crew's unplanned hostage. What had begun as a beautiful spring morning had ended as a nightmare and with me left for dead.

I experienced several moments of consciousness; I saw vague images of police and EMT's hovering over me while someone pulled back my eyelids and shined a light in my eyes. I heard someone shouting in the distance, "I have constriction of his pupils, let's move people."

Someone pushed a breathing mask over my face and secured it roughly around my head. Something stung my arm through my shirt. I heard, "Squeeze the bag hard. Get that fluid in him." Someone pulled at my clothes, searching my pockets and taking my wallet. I heard someone call my name. "Mr. DeLuca! Can you hear me?"

My eyes fluttered in response as someone pressed hard on my wound to slow the bleeding.

"Mr. DeLuca, Mr. DeLuca. Squeeze my hand if you can hear me."

I offered no reaction. My last memory of the day was two guys lifting me onto a gurney and voices yelling, "Get Eden on the radio. Tell them to have the O.R. ready. We're coming in hot!"

Three

Awake

"Abby!" I heard myself calling her name repeatedly until I realized I was sitting up, awake, and totally disoriented. Having no idea where I was, panic and anxiety arose, and my heart pounded. I thought it would explode through the wall of my chest. I'm sure you've felt as I do now at least once in your life, those few seconds of fear and insecurity leading to panic and a full-blown anxiety attack.

I lay back on the slightly raised bed as the fog that clouded my mind finally lifted. Steady beeps came from somewhere outside my consciousness, like they were not in the same room. My vision cleared, and the dizziness slowed, as did my breathing. The room materialized into solid form. I noticed the grid pattern of the rectangular ceiling tiles and the obnoxiously bright florescent light above my bed.

Something covered my nose and mouth. Both felt dry and uncomfortable, and something was attached to my left index finger. It felt like someone had placed a clothespin there as a gag to see if I would react in some strange way so the prankster could get it on video. I felt claustrophobic enclosed in this fogginess of uncertainty. With great effort, I tried to lift my head and pull the oxygen mask from my face, but the dizziness returned with a vengeance, so much so that I had no choice but to stop moving. The room spun as my head lolled back on its own. I have no control of my body, and I don't like it. I have never liked not being in control. Yes, it is one of the matching items in a complete set of baggage that comes standard issue with Paolo DeLuca, control freak. If I just lie here for a few moments, things would settle down and I could regain control.

"Just stay still . . . relax . . . breath . . ."

"Use what you know."

I forced my head off the thin pillow, and nausea welled up like a great ocean wave about to crash on a beach. I almost puked, but nothing came from a stomach that I now thank God was empty. I closed my eyes. Sleep found me a willing partner in its search for rest.

When I woke again, the room was dark. Soft lighting had replaced the harsh overhead lights, and the beeps from the machine were slow and rhythmic. I stayed still for a long time before I decided to attempt another look around. Finally, I found the courage to move my head, first side to side and then, as if putting my chin on my chest, I looked toward my feet. Realization set in as I reached with my right hand toward the oblong box tethered to the wall behind me. I pressed the buttons, hoping to find one that alerted someone that I was awake. The wall TV blared with a startling sound and just as suddenly it went off. I pressed it several more times before the door moved. And the hallway light revealed a figure entering. It was an eternity before she spoke as her portly figure wobbled to the side of my bed with exaggerated slowness in her gait.

She turned on the table lamp at the side of the bed, which cast a soft glow on everything in the room. I saw a small, round woman whose gray hair was pulled high into a bun so tight that her frown lines had all but disappeared.

"Good evening Mr. DeLuca," she said quietly, "We've been waiting for you to come back to us. How are you feeling?"

"What a stupid question! How do you think I'm feeling?" "Not sure yet."

She checked my vitals and watched the monitor, "That's to be expected."

"Where am I? I don't understand what's happening."

"You're at Eden General Mr. DeLuca."

I still had no idea where that was. I don't remember hearing anything about Eden General. I rubbed my face, trying to move along the mental fogginess faster than it was on its own.

"Where?"

"Eden General, Mr. DeLuca." And then she saw I was still confused. "You're in the critical care unit. Been here for some time now. Thought we lost you a time or two, but the good doctor and the Creator had other plans for you."

"How long?"

She took too long to answer as she fussed with the bag hanging from the metallic pole beside the bed.

"I've notified the doctor that you're awake. He'll give you . . ."

"How fucking long?" I shouted at her pudgy, round face.

"Thirteen days. You're lucky to be alive, Mr. Deluca." In her head, I could see she added, *"Asshole."*

"Where's Abby?"

"Who."

"Abby, my fiancée. I want to see her." Then I repeated for my demand, "I want to see her now!"

"I'll see what's keeping the doctor," She turned and left the room to avoid another boisterous demand.

"You better find Abby for me, fat ass!"

Anxiety loomed inside me. This whole situation didn't feel right; this didn't feel like I would get any answers, let alone the ones I wanted. I pressed the button on the pad again and again, final holding it down, as if it would help. No response. I kept pressing, and after what seemed like an eternity, I grabbed the pad and threw it in anger. When it reached the full length of its wire, it slammed on the floor and it shattered. Nurse Fat-Ass and everyone else at Eden General had their own idea of when a doctor would answer my questions, and that was *no time soon.*

What seemed like hours later, a food tray arrived and the young lady placed it on the rolling bed table. Nurse Fat-Ass must have ordered it for me. Pissed from stewing in my angry self-pity, I swiped at the tray and sent it tumbling over the end of the bed, spilling soup, tea, milk, and some other watery goo that patients are fed after not eating solids for several days. The girl exploded into tears and ran from the room. Seems like I wasn't the only one having a bad day. I wanted to yell some smartass remark about crying over spilt milk, but condensed it to a boisterous sentence starting with the *"F"* word. I needed to regain control of my emotions and figure out what was going on with me and Eden General.

I must have dozed off from my tiring outburst, or more likely from Nurse Portly spiking the fluids bag. The sun peeking through the almost shut mini blinds cast a faint glow across the shadows of the sparsely decorated room. Enough morning light shone into the room for me to read the white board hanging on the closet door facing the bed. "DUTY NURSE: M. MONAHAN, RN" The next line announced the nurse in charge was "J. UM WONG." Sometime during the night, whoever takes care of menial hospital tasks had replaced the nurse call pad. I pulled it close to me and pressed the nurse call button. Several minutes later a short, pixy-like woman entered the room.

"Good morning Mr. DeLuca. Hope you had a good night's sleep and are in a better mood. If not, I can get the restraints and make sure your breakfast doesn't end up on the floor like your dinner did. Understand me?"

I regarded her non-intimidating size and spoke with a deliberate softness. "Well, A, I had no choice but to sleep, and B, I promise to be a good boy." I raised my two fingers showing the boy scout pledge, "Scout's honor."

She smiled, "Now, what is it you need?"

"I would like to see my fiancée, Abby. If you can get ahold of her and tell her where I'm at, I would be very appreciative, Miss . . .?"

"Margaret Monahan. I'm one of your RN's.

"Oh. A great Irish Catholic name. And probably formally Catholic educated too."

"Yep. Bishop Gillespie High School for Girls, and then, Holy Family University. So, what's it to you?"

"I chuckled, "Similar up-brining, that's all. Can I call you Margaret?"

"It's Nurse Monahan, thank you."

"Thank you, Nurse Monahan. "Now, can you get Abby for me?"

She looked to be at a loss for a response and then left in mid-sentence, "I'll see what I can do."

Just before noon, the doctor entered for his late morning rounds, escorted by others who I assumed were plain-clothes police officers. I bet the delay in the doctor's rounds was due to the police's arrival. I'm sure the first call this morning, after the nurse informed the doctor that I was asking questions, was to the police, and that is why they are here now.

The doctor grabbed the chart from the slot on the wall and asked those stupid medical questions doctors always ask, like, "On a scale of one to ten, how's your pain level this morning?" And, "How do you feel?"

I had to respond with just as stupid of an answer, "I feel like somebody fucking shot me!"

He huffed something under his breath and told the nurse to "continue treatment as usual. Any changes, call me." He turned and started to leave.

"I have some questions, Doc, before you leave."

He turned with his head hung, as if I were a pestering child asking *why* repeatedly.

"What is it you want to know, Mr. DeLuca?"

"I'd love to know what's happening, and why I've been here for so long. I think I'm entitled to know and why you haven't gotten a hold of Abby like I've asked numerous times."

He exhaled with such deep disrespect that even the cops looked at each other. "Mr. DeLuca, when you were shot, the bullet nicked an artery in your leg, and the gut shot didn't help your condition. Most of your medical issues are from the massive blood loss from your system. The damage from being shot twice was minor compared to the loss of blood." He also said that I had been in a coma, probably because of the blood loss. "I think you found somewhere . . . comfortable you wanted to stay, Mr. DeLuca. There really is no other medical explanation than that for you," he paused for a few moments, "*sleeping* so long."

"So, what you're saying is that I didn't want to wake up and face reality?" That's really a load of bullshit Doc. You guys just don't want to get sued!" After that, I laid into him pretty hard about the state of today's medical care, as if it was his fault, and then blasted him for being so uncaring.

He turned to leave and eyed the officers, "He's all yours Detectives!"

One lawman spoke up after witnessing my harassment of Doctor Whoever. He introduced himself when he had entered, I just don't remember it.

"Mr. DeLuca, I'm Special agent McGregor, and this is Special Agent Lee. We're with the Philadelphia FBI Field office."

"Yeah . . . So, I'm supposed to be impressed? Do you have some credentials to show me, or am I supposed to take your word that you are who you say you are?"

McGregor removed his antiquated black leather bi-fold wallet from his inner suit jacket pocket and flipped it between his picture and his credential with what can only be described as years of experience.

"Agent Lee and I are investigating the Franklin Bank robbery. We'd like to ask you a few questions."

"That's make three of us."

"Mr. DeLuca, what is your relationship with Miss Abhijishya Woo?"

"Really? Is *that* your first question? Abby is my fiancé."

"What else can you tell us about her?"

"You mean like, is she a good cook? Or is she great in the sack? Listen and understand this question, Agent McGregor. Where the fuck is Abby?"

The young agent spoke for the first time. "We don't know Miss Woo's whereabouts. We're thinking you and she . . ."

"No, no, no, no, no! We didn't do anything pal! Now, where the hell is Abby?"

Senior Agent McGregor took over the conversation again. "We don't know where she is, Mr. DeLuca. We're assuming this is a bank heist gone bad, and it may have turned into a kidnapping. However, the bank robbers have not demanded any ransom from her parents, Mr. and Mrs. Rubin, a very wealthy couple. That is why we have some . . . very sensitive questions for your, Mr. DeLuca, concerning her disappearance.

"Yeah, well . . . I've got some fucking questions for you too! First, Abby had nothing to do with what happened at the bank, and I would never hurt her, or do anything to cause her harm. Now you tell me where the hell she is! And don't give me that, *we don't know* bullshit! You're FBI, you fucking guys know everything.

"We're FBI," Lee said, "Not CIA."

McGregor gave his partner the evil eye. "Lee, give us a minute, will you?"

The junior FBI agent left the room in a huff.

"Mr. DeLuca . . . Mr. DeLuca," The senior FBI agent called my name twice to get my attention. "What were you and Miss Woo doing at the bank at the time of the robbery?"

Exhaling deeply, I told him the story about me and Abby putting some papers into her deposit box, and about her adoption, and her search for her birth parents. I didn't say anything about the necklace hoping to draw something out, something like how much they knew or suspected. I didn't mention anything about the flash drive either. That was my little secret for now.

During his repetitive monologue of non-information, I thought of using the thumb-drive as leverage, it was the crook's original goal in the robbery, and maybe I could use it a bargaining chip. I could see myself trading the drive for Abby, and maybe the necklace at some predetermined location agreed upon by me and the thieves.

McGregor said that there had been no communication from the crew that destroyed the banks first floor. Kidnapping's meant ransom, and ransom meant money, and lots of it, which the Rubins had. With no demands for any cash, that meant the only thing they could want was the flash drive for whatever information it held. It must be something important or they would not have gone through so much trouble to get it. Or, maybe right now, they aren't sure who, if anyone, has it. Maybe they think it was destroyed during the firefight at the bank, or maybe they think the police have it.

Agent McGregor broke my train of thought when he spoke. "So, let me sum this up, Mr. DeLuca. What I hear you saying is that nothing went missing from Miss Woo's deposit box during the robbery. However, the owner of the only other box in the vault that the suspects touched has signed a sworn statement saying they had not placed anything in their box yet, which leaves Miss Woo's box as the target. That's why I'm thinking something of great value must've been in there, something so valuable that the thieves would only target two deposit boxes out of all those boxes in the vault. I'm thinking something expensive, like jewelry . . . possibly, some high dollar item the bank manager could have tipped the robbers off about. What do you think of that plausible scenario, Mr. DeLuca?"

"Listen to me closely. And get this through your thick government pea-sized brain. Her deposit box contained papers; papers she thought might lead to discovering her birth parents. That's all the fuck was in there. Nothing else!" A few heartbeats passed and then I continued. "If all they were after was whatever was in Abby's box, then why open the other box? Why target an empty box, Agent? Or aren't you guys bright enough to think of that? Maybe you should be looking at someone else for this, maybe someone who is an actual thief."

Agent Lee reentered the room, looking disappointed as he eyed McGregor, "Nothing," was all he said.

Special Agent McGregor sighed. "Mr. DeLuca, we believe that Miss Stone, the bank manager, was somehow involved in the robbery. We found highly unusual documentation on her personal laptop. Normally banks do not maintain inventory of their customer's safety deposit boxes because of implications of impropriety, yet, she did. It was a list of everything contained within every single deposit box in the vault. How did she acquire this information, and why she chose to keep it are questions we cannot answer?"

"Unless she planned the whole thing," Lee Interjected. "I'm thinking her crew turned independent, killed her, and took the prize for themselves."

"And what prize would that be?" I asked, already knowing the answer.

McGregor opened the worn, brown FBI folder he had been holding during this entire conversation and flashed me a photo of Abby's necklace. "We found this photograph in Miss Stone's home, and, according to a list of contents, also found in her home, deposit box six-oh-six, Miss Woo's box, contained a one-of-a-kind inverted tear-drop-diamond dragon necklace on a twenty-four-inch gold chain. Even more unique was its color, a cool blue. Worth millions, I'm told.

"Never seen it," I said trying to sound convincing.

"Anyway, Computer Logic, the owners of the other box-their CEO have signed a sworn statement saying they had not yet placed anything in their deposit box, nor did they intend to until the end of next week. That statement agrees with Miss Stone's, 'unofficial' inventory. Now, Mr. DeLuca, I have it here in black and white that Woo's box contained a necklace worth almost five million dollars. We spoke with the man from the diamond exchange who appraised the necklace. He said that Stone had made the appointment for Miss Woo, and Miss Stone had asked him personally to appraise it . . . as a favor for a valued customer- in her words, he told us, 'a *close friend.*' Now, Mr. Deluca, do you still want to insist that the necklace was not in the box when you and Miss Woo were in the vault just as the robbery began?"

"Agent McGregor, does the FBI require you guys to get annual fucking hearing exams? I fucking told you; no necklace was in the box. Do you understand? Or do I need to write it down and pin it to your lapel?"

The two agents exchanged glances of anger.

"Alright, Mr. DeLuca," Agent McGregor said returning the necklace photo to the folder, closing it, and placing it under his arm. "We checked the clothes you came in wearing and, your personal belongings, and, as Lee here has said, nothing was in them. I don't know how, yet, but I think you somehow had time to hide the necklace before passing out. Sooner or later, Mr. DeLuca, I'll figure you out."

"Who the hell gave you permission to check my belongings?" You didn't present a warrant, and you didn't ask my permission."

"Mr. DeLuca, if you continue to deny that the necklace was in Miss Woo's and your possessions while the two of you were at the bank, I'll have to treat you as a suspect in Miss Woo's disappearance, and as someone with ties to Miss Stone. I can make a case where you and Miss Stone colluded and set up Miss Woo to gain her trust so the two of you could steal the necklace. After all, Mr. DeLuca, you've only known Miss Woo a short time, about the same amount of time Miss Stone has been manager of the Franklin Bank branch that was robbed. I can also charge you with conspiracy to murder Miss Stone and her children. In reality, I can charge you with whatever the hell I want to unless you start to cooperate. What do you have to say about that, Mr. DeLuca?"

"On what charge? Theft of an unofficial item from an unofficial inventory by a woman who was obviously under duress and probably conspiring on the theft. I was in the vault, asshole! I was there when it all went down. Hello . . . witness! You guys have not been listening. Let me say this slowly enough so even government agents can understand. No necklace was in the box Agent McGregor. Do I need to repeat it again for you Agent Lee? And again, you had no legal right to search my belongings, unless you have a warrant you haven't shown me yet."

It was silent in the room until I spoke again, "I want to contact a lawyer, I feel you're violating my civil rights." I contemplated how Lee missed the drive tucked into the tiny pocket of my jeans, unless he found it and was hiding it from McGregor.

McGregor looked at Lee and then in my direction. "Mr. DeLuca, I'll obtain a federal warrant to search your property and everything else you may own, even the property you have registered in you dead father's name at the old navy yard. I'll crawl so far up your ass that I'll be able to tell your doctor about the condition of your colon. I will also return with an arrest warrant charging you for Miss Woo's disappearance and kidnapping, the theft of her property, and the murder of Miss Stone and her children. I can even level a trespassing charge since you yourself didn't have an account at the bank, and any other charges I can think of that will ruin you and your reputation for life, even if they are not true. Do you get me Mr. DeLuca?"

I spoke calmly, like we had never argued, just like Abby had taught me to do, think first, then speak.

"I do. Now get the fuck out!"

"As you wish Mr. DeLuca; however, we will return within the hour with a warrant for . . ."

"Get the fuck out!"

They left the room faster than I thought the old man could move. I lay down and closed my eyes; I was tired from all the confrontation. I took deep breaths to calm my heart rate causing the monitor to beep at a rapid pace.

It couldn't have been more than thirty seconds before a male voice broke the machine's rhythmic chirping, "Mr. DeLuca?"

I opened my eyes, "Can't you guys take a fucking hint? I told you two to leave me the fuck alone," as I turned my head toward the door of the darkening room.

Two different people stood in the doorway holding up leather-bound placards and badges. "Mr. DeLuca, we are United States Federal Marshalls. We'd like to speak with you about Miss Abhijishya Woo . . ."

"What the fuck!" I began to wonder what Abby had gotten herself involved in. This was a lot of attention for a bank robbery. I could see the FBI's involvement, but the United States Marshalls? "Damn, Abby, What the hell did you do?"

Four

United States Marshals

"Can't you guys give it a rest? Your friends were just in here, asking all kinds of bullshit questions about Abby. Just what the hell do you expect me to tell you that I didn't already tell them?" Their heads swiveled between each other and then toward me.

With confusion in his voice, the older man spoke again, "Mr. DeLuca, there must be some misunderstanding. We are here about Miss Abhijishya Woo and the Franklin Bank robbery. We don't know anything about . . . our friends . . ." His voice trailed into silence.

"Come on, man! Jesus Christ! Didn't you see them in the hallway? Are you guys blind as well as deaf? Christ! I can't believe this bullshit day."

They regarded each other, silently asking if I was as crazy as I sounded.

"Mr. DeLuca, can we start again? I'm Marshal Samuel Diego, and this is my partner, Marshal Jane Brennan. We're here about the disappearance of Miss Woo. We need to know about your involvement in our case."

"Involvement in your case? I don't know a damn thing about your case." I was angry again. Loud, angry, and ready to pounce on anyone who pissed me off. That is one of my demons, the inability to tolerate the stupidity of people in authority. I have my reasons for this, and, in the past, it plagued my military career.

"Mr. DeLuca, our office out of Dallas has just assigned us this case, well, a reassignment for me anyway," He paused to collect his thoughts. Our office has tasked Marshal Brennan and I with finding the whereabouts of Miss Woo. We haven't been able to contact her, and she is overdue for her monthly check in."

"Monthly check in? What the hell are you guys talking about? And why is she involved with the Marshal service?"

"The situation required Miss Woo to verbally check in monthly with our office, but she missed her scheduled call-in time several times now. When we inquired with the local authorities, we learned about her involvement with the bank robbery, so our supervisors have dispatched us to Philadelphia to see what happened to her."

"Really guys, I'm at a loss here. Abby was not involved in anything. We went to the bank to put some papers in her safety deposit box, papers she hoped would help her find her birth parents. Whatever this other shit is, is bullshit. Just what do you think Abby is involved in?"

The agents looked just as lost as I was; they talked at the same time, and then Brennan touched Diego's elbow and spoke to him in a soft calming voice. "Let me try boss." She walked farther into the room from the confines of the blue steel doorframe. "Mr. DeLuca, again, I'm Marshal Jane Brennan. I think we have some information you need to hear concerning Miss Woo. First, may I ask, how long have you known her?"

I tried my best to match the softness of Brennan's voice with the quietness of my own. "I've known Abby for over six months." Saying it out loud like that, being blunt with those words for the first time, made it sound like I was looking for approval from her concerning the short-term relationship between me and Abby. Pushing the thought of her disapproval from my mind, I changed the direction of the questions from her to me, to me to them. "I have about a million questions for you, about all of this." I gestured to the room and to the world in general.

"First, I don't understand what the hell is happening here, with all the carnage at the bank, the robbery, with Abby." My voice broke and trembled for the first time realizing that I may never see Abby again. I spoke louder just to break the fear emanating from my voice. "What the hell is going on?"

Brennan continued to try to resume calmness to the room. "Mr. DeLuca, please bear with me. Let me explain some things to you. The federal government has charged our agency with protecting Miss Woo since she was about six months old. Now I admit, this seems extremely unusual, that her case is the longest ongoing protection detail in the agency's history . . . and that it has been almost twenty-five years, and additionally, our office has assigned six different marshals since its inception. So, Mr. DeLuca, what I'm trying to ask you is, did Miss Woo ever tell you that she was in the witness protection program?"

My dumb, blank stare must have answered the question, and I confirmed its meaning with, "No. She *never* said anything about contacting anyone or any agency, on any kind of schedule."

Brennan waited.

"If someone is in witness protection, why would they tell someone? And if they did, wouldn't that defeat the purpose of being in witness protection?"

She looked at Diego as if asking permission from the senior agent to explain something so simple to someone so clueless. He gave her permission with a silent nod. "Mr. DeLuca. Can I call you Paolo?"

"Only my mother calls me Paolo. You can call me *Mr. DeLuca*." I was still was angry at their continued intrusion into my relationship with Abby, and angry about everything I suddenly didn't know about her.

"Okay, Mr. DeLuca. Here's the short version. Miss Woo's parents came to the States seeking political asylum. The Chinese government employed them as microbiologists . . . specializing in chemical weaponry. The Woos fled China when they learned that Mrs. Woo was pregnant with a female offspring. Even though the Chinese government has eased up on the one-child policy, they still frown upon female children, especially in this case."

"Why?"

"Look, I can only tell you what's in the file, so listen quietly please. Mrs. Woo didn't want an abortion, and Mr. Woo agreed. If their superiors discovered the baby's gender, they would have forced the abortion and blamed it on Chinese tradition."

"All this is in the file?"

"May I finish?"

I rolled my eyes in response.

"The Woos made their way to the U. S. Embassy, and the U.S. granted them asylum for exchange of information about China's chemical weapons program, which they willingly agreed to."

"So how did they fall under the protection of the United States Marshals?"

"Well, from what I can surmise from the file, a very loose interpretation of the Crimes against Humanities clause and a sympathetic president. I believe it was all politically motivated deep state stuff. To conclude, Mr. DeLuca, the program originally located them to Lufkin, Texas."

"Sounds like a real dump. No offense, Brennan."

"None taken. Texas isn't for everyone. The last thing mentioned in the file was their employment. Our office placed them in jobs at a government contractors lab called ChemCor, a subdivision of Computer Logic Systems."

"Computer Logic?" I blurted out with more emotion than I wanted to.

"Yeah, that was the parent company's name. Why do you ask?"

I looked at the two marshals, amazed they hadn't made the connection.

"You just spent ten minutes telling me every detail of the life and times of the Woos, and their daughter, and you don't see this?"

"See what Mr. DeLuca? Why don't you enlighten us with what you think we're missing?" Diego spoke with a snide tone, hinting at who were the seasoned lawmen here.

"Computer Logic was the name of the company that also had their deposit box broken into at the bank. The one the FBI said was empty, the one the company swore they never put anything into. *HELLO!* The one they killed the manager over after she opened it for them."

The Marshals exchanged a silent worried glance before Diego spoke. "Mr. DeLuca, we need to place you into protective custody until we figure out just what the hell is happening here."

"No fucking way! The nurse told me I've been here thirteen days, and its way to long for Abby not to be in real trouble. I need to find her; I need to know she's still alive. I need to . . ."

"The crew that robbed the bank know what you look like, Mr. DeLuca," Marshal Brennan interrupted. "And they may know who you are. You can't help anyone if you are dead."

Her words hit me hard enough to hurt, like a bar of soap in a sock. Something I wasn't familiar with, but she made her point damn clear. I could not help Abby if I was dead."

Diego unsuccessfully looked for my clothes in the closet.

"The hospital may still have them," I said. That jackass Agent Lee from the FBI had gone through them earlier today. My clothes are at the nurse's station where he left them after searching through them."

"I'll check. Get ready to move as soon as I get back." Diego said. He looked at Brennan to assure that I would be ready.

I sat upright, still a bit woozy. I was hoping to walk right out of here, even after lying in bed for so long, but I'm sure they would help me if I couldn't manage under my own power.

Diego quickly returned and tossed a plastic bag at me, "Get dressed."

I ripped open the bag and sorted through my clothes. The pants were shredded having been cut off in the emergency room, and the shirt was blood stained, making everything useless. "I need some other clothes. I may look out of place without wearing anything while we're walking out of here." Brennan ran from the room to find something.

"Why the hell would they even keep this stuff?" I asked Diego.

"The duty nurse said the agents instructed her to keep them for evidence when they brought you into the emergency room, which they did. She also said no one ever came for them."

I didn't question it. I know from experience that shit gets jumbled in the confusion of the emergency room.

Brennan returned moments later with a complete set of scrubs and a paper mask; she had commandeered from some unseen storage closet. "Put this on, Doctor DeLuca.," she teased as she tossed the soft blue clothing at me.

All that time in bed proved difficult for me to stand on my own. Diego helped me up until the dizziness passed as I stubbornly protested his aid.

"We don't have time for any macho bullshit DeLuca."

I removed my hospital gown and stood there in all my glory. Diego turned away, but Brennan just watched with no hint of emotion on her face, or in her eyes.

I dressed as quickly as I could and sat in the hard-plastic blue chair meant to force visitors to not stay so long. I slipped on a pair of those funky blue rubber-soled socks because my shoes were nowhere to be found.

"That'll do for now, DeLuca, and the socks match your eyes," Brennan chuckled while trying to insult my manhood.

Diego patted my back, "Yeah, they're so you, DeLuca."

Nurse Portly entered the room just as I finished dressing., "And just where do you think you're going Mr. DeLuca?"

Diego pulled her aside and told her softly that they were taking me into protective custody.

"But . . ." she began.

I heard him concoct some phony law statute, and quote some federal-sounding numbers that probably meant nothing to anyone. She still protested, telling the marshal how the FBI had told her and security that I was not allowed to leave the hospital under any circumstances. She gave Diego the same rash of shit he had given her.

Brennan got involved and grabbed the nurse by the identification lanyard hanging from her neck. She pulled her close and glared into her eyes as she spoke with just enough mock anger to scare a full, grown man. "Listen up, sweetheart, if you don't shut your fucking mouth, I'll charge you with obstruction of justice, threating a law enforcement officer, interfering with law enforcement officers in performance of their duty, and any other bullshit charge I can fabricate so you're locked up for at least seventy-two hours. Do you understand me?" Brennan pushed her hard against the steel door frame to drive the point home. That was more than enough to quiet Nurse Portly's protest.

While that one-sided conversation was transpiring, I had slid my hand into the thin pocket of my former jeans, and retrieved the flash drive. I kept it in my hand as I tossed the jeans into the trash. I hadn't mentioned the flash drive to the marshals, and I had no plan to.

As Brennan continued to stare down the nurse, Diego pulled me from the chair. He was ready to leave, and so was I. Brennan let the nurse leave, and now the three of us were ready to move.

Brennan hung Nurse Protly's ID around my neck, "It complements your ensemble." I didn't see her take it from the nurse during the intimidation session at the doorway, but Brennan was right, it made me look official, and with it, I could hide in plain sight.

Diego told us to wait just inside the door while he checked the hallway for any other unforeseen obstructions. Meanwhile, I realized I didn't really understand the whole witness protection story. If Abby was in the program, why would she try to find her parents, let alone contact anyone who may have known them. Those actions would reveal who she was, and where she was. I also wondered if her foster parents knew about it, maybe they did, and I'm just assuming they didn't. Or, maybe the check-ins were part of some on-going government adoption process. Too many questions didn't have answers, like, how was Abby involved with ChemCor and Computer Logic? And, for my own selfishness, who *was* Abby? That was the most important question I needed answered.

I need to get my head right if I was going to find out anything, or be able to help Abby. I pushed the last thought from my mind as I sat again just as Diego entered the room.

"What the hell are you doing DeLuca? Get up. We need to go! Now!"

"I'm not moving until you answer some more questions."

"We don't have time for this bullshit."

"I've got time."

"Christ. Make them short questions, DeLuca," Diego said.

"Okay, how did the Woos end up in Philadelphia? It's a long way from Assbutt Texas."

Diego spoke fast, like the guy who narrates the disclaimer on some television ad. "Mrs. Woo wasn't happy in Texas. With Mrs. Woo unhappy, Mr. Woo was miserable, and he became uncooperative. Woo told the man in charge that unless he moved them somewhere with a little more tolerable climate, like Pennsylvania, neither him, nor his wife would continue to work or give them any more information. So, here we are, DeLuca. Can we go now?"

"Last question. Why weren't full-time custodial duties of the Woos transferred to the Philadelphia Marshals office? Seems like it should have been a no brainer, geographically speaking.

"I can't answer that, DeLuca."

"Can't. Or Won't Marshal?"

"Can't," Diego said harshly. "That's all above my pay grade. Now let's go . . . please."

I stood up ready to do as the marshal asked. "I'm all yours."

FIVE

The Parents Of

On a scale of one to ten, today was a minus two and heading down-hill with the speed of a snow avalanche. First up was this bullshit with the FBI, and then this on-going confrontation with the Marshal Service. They were intent with taking me into protective custody, and I was just as intent at not going, but I told them I would agree to go, since they had answered some of my questions. More importantly, they were a way out of the hospital. Now, to top off everything else, as we were about to leave the room, Abby's parents entered. Diego uttered several choice words, provoking an array of nasty looks from Abby's mother.

With their appearance, the numerical day-rating number plummeted to a negative ten with a bullet. Nurse Portly had told me earlier today, in forced polite conversation, that they had visited the hospital almost every day, asking for an update on my condition. Because of their credentials, they were kept in the loop as to my recovery process. I never held anything against them no matter how often they insulted me, it was their way, intentional or not. They spoke plainly from the heart, and they were two parents wholly concerned for their daughter's well-being, nothing else.

Mr. and Mrs. Rubin- (actually Doctor and Doctor Rubin) are a deeply religious Jewish couple. Like Abraham and Sarah from the Old Testament, they could not have children of their own, so they adopted Abby. As her parents, they insisted she find and follow a religion, no matter what faith it may be. They felt that a formal religious structure would help her cope with not knowing who her birth parents were. Her adoption was not a family secret. The reason was obvious, Abby looked nothing like the Rubins. They both wanted a child to fill the void, Abby did that for them. Of course, Abby refused to follow anything she thought too intrusive on her time, or would deter from her search for her parents. She had no time for religion, no matter how emphatic her parents were on the subject.

During those times, and there have been only few when I had met the Rubins, I could see the love they had for each other and for Abby. They would have loud conversations about everyday things, like which kitchen drawer the aluminum foil should be in. Mr. Rubin would put it in the dish towel drawer, and then Mrs. Rubin would move it to the drawer with the plastic grocery bags. Mr. Rubin would put his foot down and say something was final, and the Mrs. Rubin would agree and do it her way anyway.

She always let Mr. Rubin think he got his way and that he was in charge, but the truth was that Mrs. Rubin always made the final decision. She always had the last word, even when she didn't utter a sound. Sometimes her face would say all that needed to be said. After the spirited conversations, Mrs. Rubin would give her husband a tight hug, a kiss on the cheek, and all would be forgiven. It had finally dawned on me that Abby acted the same way with me, firm, strong, opinionated, and, most of all . . . loving.

Being a strong woman in the Rubin family appeared to be one trait Abby had learned from her step-mother. I love that about her, she'll speak her mind no matter the consequences.

I had just finished dressing, had stood from the chair and was almost to the door when the Rubins entered the room with Mrs. Rubin leading the way. She forced Diego back inside, which was the reason he started his foul rant. I tried to hide my *oh shit* expression as Mr. Rubin spoke with an accusatory tone projecting from his short stature frame.

"Where's my daughter? What have you gotten her involved in? So, help me, if Abby is hurt I will . . ."

Mrs. Rubin said something in Hebrew to him; he went silent and lowered his head in exasperated fashion.

Diego and Brennan excused themselves from the room. Diego regarded the three of us as he spoke, "We don't have time for this."

Mrs. Rubin looked directly at Brennan as the marshals passed her on the way to the hallway. I saw a look of disgust and disapproval on her face, which she had no intention of hiding.

Once the marshals were in the hallway, Mrs. Rubin said, "Please excuse my husband. He's been like this since Abby was taken. We came as soon as the nurse called and told us you were awake. Now tell me, how are you feeling?"

She saw my hesitation at the unexpected question of concern. Her daughter was missing, and she was asking how I felt. It's not how I would have begun the conversation if the tables were turned.

When I didn't answer right away, she said, "Paolo," with an unexpected softness, "Let's put everything else aside for now. Except for Abby. Will you be okay with that?" She placed her hand on my shoulder in a reassuring gesture, like a mother comforting a child.

Only my mother calls me Paolo, but Mrs. Rubin was a mother after all, a Jewish mother, need I say more? As a mother she recognized the pain on my face when her husband asked about Abby. Maybe she also felt the anguish I kept deep inside since I could not help Abby on the day of the robbery.

Even though Mrs. Rubin always got her way, I told her, "Everyone calls me *DeLuca* . . . but it's okay with me if you call me *Paolo*."

Looking at Abby's stepfather, and trying to maintain the appearance of being the alpha male and the bigger man, I answered the question Mrs. Rubin had asked about putting things aside. "I can, if he will." My voice broke at the end of my statement at the memory of the same conversation I had with my own father.

Mr. Rubin started to say something, but his wife cut him short with, "He will." It was an agreement to my request, and an order to put his disapproving I'm her father position aside until Abby was safe at home. She also gave him a look of *I dare you to say different.* It was clear Mrs.

Rubin was in charge today, and there would be no saying anything different, by either Mr. Rubin or myself.

Now that all the male posturing was out of the way, Mrs. Rubin started over with, "How are you feeling Paolo?"

She sounded so much like my mother, and that's why I opened up, and told her how I was really feeling. It was probably the first time I was open and truthful since I had first met them.

I could not look her in the eye as I told her, "I feel . . . lost without Abby." If I had looked at her, I knew I would have cried, something my father said a man never should do.

Mr. Rubin took advantage of the silence and lifted his head, and I could see he was on the verge of tears. He started to speak, and Mrs. Rubin said something again to him in Hebrew. I didn't understand its meaning, but I knew what it implied. He replied something I know he would not normally do, but these were not normal times for any of us.

He regarded me with fierce anger in his eyes just behind the tears, "No matter what my wife says, Mr. DeLuca, our Abby is missing, and you are to blame. If you didn't encourage her the way you did, she would be here now, safe with her family."

Mrs. Rubin yelled at him this time, "Leon, you promised you would not do this now! Can't you see this is not helping anyone?"

He retorted in what I can only describe as Yiddish. The two argued in a language I didn't understand, but, from its tone, I knew it was about me. If Abby were here, she would know what to say to get them to stop arguing.

Mrs. Rubin spoke in English again, "The Creator would be ashamed of you Leon!"

Mr. Rubin shrugged his shoulders, "Ah, I'm sure he knows why I feel this way, and I don't think he'll mind that I am defending the welfare of my daughter."

Abby had once tried to explain the Jewish faith to me, as she understood it. She said that Jewish people use the word *Hashem* (The Name) or, *Yahweh* (I am) when referring to God, the Creator. It was a deep and respectful tradition not to refer to the Creator by the name, God. Abby also told me their story of Moses and how it differed from my Roman Catholic upbringing. I always suspected the Rubin's religion and my background were a source of tension between the Rubins, Abby, and me.

"Paolo, when Abby brought you home and told us of some of your past, we were . . . unhappy, to say the least. But we know that Abby is not a Jewish woman and never will be, even though my husband still holds out hope. She brought you to our home, and we saw a man who did not practice a religion, any religion, and did not have a steady job. What were we to think, or do? How could we give our blessing to a man who has no spiritual guidance? How could he take care of our Abby? And, how could you suggest she get a tattoo?" If she were Catholic, she would have crossed herself as she spoke those words. "You know the history of the death camps, the Jews, the Nazis, the numbers placed on the arms of millions of innocent people. And most of all, how could a good man ask our daughter to give up all she had worked for, to chase a dream? This we do not understand, Paolo!"

I stayed quiet the entire time Mrs. Rubin chastised me. "I understand your questions and concerns, Mrs. Rubin, but right now, I have no answers for you."

She held it together better than I was and she let me know how she felt about my position on religion. "Paolo, have you ever heard the saying that when people stop believing in God, they don't believe in nothing, they believe in anything? What I . . ."

Mr. Rubin harrumphed.

"Sorry Leon. What we are asking you, Paolo, is just what do you believe?"

As if on cue, with the slightest hesitation in my response, Mr. Rubin began where he left off earlier. "This is your fault! Abby was ready to finish medical school, and then you come along and mix up her mind with some fantasy. You had to butt into our lives. You had to make her change what she wanted to do! Again, I blame you, Mr. DeLuca. If I was a few years younger, I would kick your ass!"

Just like the last time we'd met; the argument became very loud. I remember Abby had gotten between us and had yelled at her father. She had never done anything like that before, and it shocked him. She was no longer his little girl, the pain on his face had spoken the silent thought in his mind. She had told him that if he didn't stop his constant criticizing and accept me for who I was, he would never see her again. That threat had hurt both of us. Neither of us men wanted to compete for Abby's love, but that was her solution for getting the arguments to stop. It had been the last straw, or a line in the sand, or whatever saying is appropriate here. It not only stopped the arguments; it had stopped any communication he and I had until this moment. Abby's mother had been there the entire time, witnessing the battel for dominance, which Abby had undoubtedly won. Abby had turned with anger and said under her breath while hiding tears from her father, "I'm done with this." We left their house in a turbulent wake of sorrow and grief with Abby leading the way. I had heard Mrs. Rubin cry-yelling at her husband, calling him a stubborn mule, telling him to go after his daughter and ask her for her forgiveness. He never followed us outside.

People are always saying that" if you don't know history, you are doomed to repeat it." Well, I got news for them, I knew this history, and I'm repeating it anyway. It was exactly like the last time we had met. The only difference this time was that I wanted it to end. I wanted it over until I could find Abby, and, when I did find her, we would all sit down and discuss their concerns.

It took great restraint, but I stood from the chair and silently extended my hand in Mr. Rubin's direction in an effort to calm the waters, a peace offering, as it may be.

He refused to take it, and cemented the refusal by spitting at my gesture.

Mrs. Rubin was visibly angry with him and his refusal at the temporary truce.

I regarded her with an *I tried* expression, hoping for some reassurance. She gave me a tight hug and whispered, "Please forgive him Paolo. He misses Abby terribly."

I wiped at my eyes, pretending I was not crying. I spoke with confidence, promising them both I would find Abby and bring her home safe.

Mrs. Rubin grabbed my hand, "And what can you do? You're just a part-time auto mechanic." And then, as an afterthought, she added, "No offense intended, Paolo." The strong matter-of-fact stereotypical Jewish mother had just emerged. She was, after all, concerned for her daughter's safety, and so was I.

"None taken. You sound just like my mother . . . no offense intended."

She smirked while probably thinking how awful a son I must be to compare something that may be offensive to my own mother. Then she did something unexpected, she hugged me tight after a kiss on my cheek, and I responded in kind.

As if on cue, Diego and Brennan entered the room, and Brennan spoke with that sweet southern Texas drawl, "Now ain't that the cutest thing you ever did see?"

Diego cut her off as she wanted to offer more commentary, "Sorry to break things up DeLuca, but we need to get moving."

Mrs. Rubin retorted in a protective tone, "And where are you taking him?"

Brennan replied with a bit too much authority in her voice, "Some place safe, Mrs. Rubin."

Mrs. Rubin looked at Brennan with daggers in her eyes, and she spoke with the same disdain in her voice, "I know what you're after. You keep your hands to yourself, Miss . . ."

"It's Marshal Brennan, and I only have a professional interest where Mr. DeLuca is concerned. I can assure you of that."

Mrs. Rubin said something in Hebrew toward Brennan, and her husband looked at her with surprise, a reaction of, *did she really just say that?*

When this is all over, I'll have to ask Mrs. Rubin what she called Brennan that invoked such an expression on her husband's face. He was surprised enough to turn a mild shade of red.

Abby's parents turned to leave, and Mrs. Rubin spoke with concern as she left the room, "Be careful out there, Paolo."

Brennan exhaled, "It's no wonder so many marshals have worked on this case. I'm betting Mrs. Rubin scared the crap out of them."

I chuckled, "I know she scares me!"

Again, Diego reminded us that it was time to get our asses in gear and that we needed to get to the safe house. Diego led us from the room and toward the closest stairwell. He told Brennan it was time they checked in with the higher ups.

"Better you than me boss!" Brennan joked, obviously knowing what was in store for Diego.

We walked as calmly as possible, trying to blend in with the walls, hoping to go unnoticed. That lasted for all of about thirty seconds, because Mrs. Rubin called after us from the nurse's station. She had cornered the duty nurse and had her backed up against the counter like she was a treed cat.

The nurse closed the chart she had been sharing with Mrs. Rubin, probably mine, then, when Mrs. Rubin faced us, the nurse ran away like her ass was on fire.

"Marshal Brennan, I want your cell-phone number, just in case I have a question or two." No, *may I have,* or, *will you please,* came from her mouth. It was a direct order from Commander Rubin.

Diego tried desperately not to smile when he told Brennan, "We'll meet you at the car after you give Mrs. Rubin your cell number," as he pulled me into the stairwell leaving Brennan the sole focus of the commander's attention.

Twenty minutes later, Brennan finally arrived and she didn't look happy. She slammed the car door in anger, and then had trouble buckling the seat-belt. Diego laughed out loud as he pulled away from the curb, "Well, how'd it go?"

Brennan returned, "Fuck you, Diego!"

Six

Safe House

I sometimes wondered, as I'm sure you have, where all of my tax dollars went, and right here before my eyes is one of the answers to that question. It was a thirty-minute ride to the safe house, during which I protested over and over that we were wasting time, time I could be using to look for Abby, and time I could be using to get things together to search for her.

Brennan scolded me like a mother blasting her child for one to many *"are we there yets?"* Then she blasted me with how late in the day it was and that it was best for all of us to get some sleep. She was probably right, but I didn't agree.

This government-issued black SUV was oversized and contained every option the manufacturer offered. Even the in-dash GPS seemed to be enjoying the ride as it ferried us to this secure location.

As we rode in luxury, I asked the marshals, "Why are you using the GPS? Don't you know where your own safe house is?"

"Again, Diego and I are both from Texas," Brennan offered. "He's been here for a full day now. I just arrived in Philadelphia prior to us meeting you at Eden General."

It was a bit of information but still didn't answer why the marshals were here from Texas; the Philly branch of law enforcement should handle this.

77

"Great, I really feel safe with two guys that have absolutely no idea where the hell they are going."

Brennan turned and smiled at me. In her most unprofessional Texas drawl, she said, "Don't ya'll fret none, cowboy. Me and Diego will show you nothing but southern hospitality. We'll keep ya'll safe and sound." She held up the biggest revolver I've ever seen, it looked like the 357 magnum Clint Eastwood had in that movie, but larger. Maybe it looked that large because of Brennan's small stature. I had a vision of her firing the weapon and flying backwards, like Yosemite Sam in a *Looney Tunes* cartoon.

"I thought a safe house was some tacky motel room. You guys must have one hell of an operations budget!" If I had to choose a descriptive word for where they are planning to keep me safe, it would be *opulent*. Halfway up the drive to the house, a tall black wrought-iron gate blocked access to the grounds. Diego opened the window and entered a four-digit code on a keypad attached to a post matching the gate's design. Inside the gate, the driveway wound through tall evergreens leading to a circular terminus where a large water fountain graced the main entrance. The fountains red brick wall matched the red curb-stone, which enhanced the driveway's black pavement and the man-size shutters adorning the house. Two solid wood entry doors led to an orbital grand parlor bookended by a marble stairway. The black and white marble floor tiles were polished to such a degree that a person could see their reflection.

"Christ, I can see myself in the tile!" I said mockingly.

"Lord almighty, this beats the Motel Six, or any other place we've ever stayed," Brennan said. "I get first pick of a suite. You know, call dibs and all before any of you boys do." Then in the best southern bell, Georgian accent I could muster, I asked, "Got anything to eat here, Diego?" I am simply famished!"

"I'll call for a pizza," Diego responded.

The marshals dropped their bags where they stood. Diego went through the doorway between the stairs while Brennan and I chatted about all the gaudy furnishings in the grand parlor entrance.

"Can't afford this place on a marshal's salary!" Brennan joked.

I agreed with her following in Diego's footsteps to the rooms beyond the parlor. In the large living room, I lay on the overstuffed dark brown couch. Brennan sat across from me and placed her now bare feet on the coffee table's glass top.

"Something doesn't add up, Brennan," I began with little sarcasm in my voice.

Brennan took a deep, deliberate breath before speaking, while trying to control her patience, "Such as, Mr. DeLuca?"

"Such as, I don't know much about witness protection, or how it's supposed to work. However, what I do know is that if Abby is under the supervision of the marshal service, then Abhijishya is not her real name. That also means that Woo is not her real last name. It's almost like I've never really known who Abby is, at least not like I thought I did. So, fill me in, Brennan. And why such a long stretch of time in the program? What's the real story?"

Brennan put her feet down onto the gray shag carpet and sat upright. She interlaced her fingers and placed her forearms on her thighs in a position of comfortable authority. "Mr. DeLuca, I'm barely up to speed on this case myself, but I'll share what I know. On the flight here, I read Woo's file, or what there is of it. Abhiji-whatever *is* her real name" Brennan said stumbling over Abby's first name. "It was part of the agreement made between her birth parents and our agency, so most of what you know about her is true."

"And?"

"And from what I could conclude from the file notes, we would place any children born to the Woos into protective custody if any harm came to the Woos themselves."

"Children? But Abby is an only child."

"Semantics, DeLuca. They drafted the agreement to include any possible future Woo children, along with the child she was carrying at the time."

"So, the Woos information on China's chemical weapons program held enough potential to force the government to agree to lifelong protection of any possible offspring? It must have been some serious shit."

"Maybe, but you know how governments are, DeLuca. They'd give away the store if they thought they could get a morsel of intel from someone, and after they're done with you, they'll stick it in your ass as hard as possible."

"Speaking from experience, Brennan?" I asked with no malice.

"Just from what I've seen in the business. I've been on the job long enough to see how those sworn to uphold the law can manipulate it to fit their best interests."

"You're dissatisfied with your current employer?"

Brennan huffed, "No, I'm just saying that in some cases, maybe like this one, with Abby and her tenure in the protection of the service, sometimes things are done for reasons that have nothing to do with the law."

"I know a little about that," I said mockingly. "Tell me more about witness protection, Brennan."

"Like what?"

"Like, how does it all work? I mean, it can't be like that shit in the movies."

Brennan made herself more comfortable on her chair. "Actually, it can. The marshal service started wit-sec back in the days of the New York mobs. There's a place in Washington D.C. used as safe space for any witness or informants, but, in Abby's case, it's not relevant. Most people in wit-sec are criminals; however, Abby is in the five percent who are not. Normally, the family doesn't get to pick where we relocate them to, but, in her file, it says we moved the Woos from Texas to Philadelphia because of Mrs. Woo's strong objections to the shithole of a town they were in."

"Does sound odd."

"Everything else checks though, the stipend we awarded, money for food and housing until they could find work, a used car that didn't stand out in the public's eye to help keep their identity safe. It's pretty self-explanatory, DeLuca."

"Except for the part where your agency moved them to Philly. Sounds to me like someone else was pulling some strings from outside the marshal's office."

Brennan exhaled with some frustration. "Yeah, maybe, but most marshals joined to serve and protect, not to babysit and buy groceries for criminals. It can leave a bad taste in your mouth."

"I've been there before, Brennan. Doing some stuff I was ordered to that I didn't think were right, or agreed with"

"Part of the job, DeLuca," she added with much frustration.

"One more question, Brennan."

"And what would that be? Brennan asked in a tone I hadn't heard before.

"What about Abby's parents? How much do they know?"

Brennan sat back on the chair and put her feet on the table. "Her adopted parents are, in

fact, in the medical field. According to her file, Abby has an IQ of one hundred and thirty-five, meaning she has superior intelligence, which is why the Rubins wanted her to go into medicine, which you already know. Abby's birth parents were Chinese scientists who asked for asylum in America, like I told you earlier. Seven months after Abby was born, her parents were killed in an automobile accident on Broad Street while in route to the navy yard."

"You keep indicating that her file isn't really informative, and yet you seem to have extensive knowledge of her. Why?"

"I thought you said one more question? This is another question, DeLuca."

"Yeah but, it's a natural response to all you have told me. You seem to know more about Abby than I do, and she is my fiancée. I'm feeling a bit left out here, Brennan."

"It's more like the file is bland, or maybe uneventful. It's almost like someone had been coaching the marshals service, trying to ensure they could get to Abby when they needed her for something. I don't know DeLuca, It's a gut thing. Something just doesn't feel right. I don't know why I'm even telling you this. It's not like you have any experience with this kind of thing."

Brennan hesitated before speaking again, "Back to your original question of what's her real story. It's left to the imagination, because no discernable answers exist. What I know is she missed several of her contact times, and someone up the chain of command wants to know why. So here we are, looking for why." Brennan's voice switched to cop mode. "The necklace you say you don't know anything about is a link to her maternal ancestry."

I remained expressionless as Brennan maneuvered around the necklace question with expertise. Abby had told me it was a family heirloom, but I wasn't going to share that with Brennan yet. "Again, you seem to know a lot of Abby's history, and yet you swear the file is bland and uninformative. Can I chalk this orientation of her life all up to good police work?"

"Diego and I are just piecing shit together here, DeLuca. I'm not saying it's fact or fiction, I'm saying it's all an analysis of our short investigation. And for the moment' it's all speculative."

"It's a hell of a lot of speculation, Brennan. Any other possible avenues you'd like to add to the story?"

"It's possible her mother was a direct descendent of the Ming Dynasty's royal family, according to the FBI's interpreter's foot-notes, believe it or not, there may be proof. After the paramedics removed you from the vault, the FBI confiscated the remaining contents of Abby's deposit box as evidence, and for analysis. Do you remember seeing any of the papers she had stored in the box?"

"No," I lied. "Not really, it looked like stuff you might find in someone's attic. I think there wasn't as much information in there as Abby hoped. She would go to the bank a few times a month, and put on . . ." I caught myself before I said *necklace* and Brennan sat upright in the chair. "She would put the papers on the table and review them. I guess looking for something she hadn't seen before."

Brennan smiled as she spoke slowly and deliberately, "She would put on, what, DeLuca? The necklace? I know you think keeping the necklaces existence a secret will somehow help you find Abby, but it wouldn't help her at all, especially if you keep lying to me about it. The necklace's value alone makes her life meaningless, and as a trained agent, Mr. DeLuca, with all due respect, Abby is probably already dead."

Brennan let that statement set in before she continued. "Unless there's something else you want to tell me. Is there anything else you want to tell me, Mr. DeLuca?"

I rubbed my palms on the scrubs pants I was still wearing hoping to remove the tension and calm myself. It gave me time to consider what and how much I should tell Brennan. Her nature made it easy to open up to her, but I've always had trust issues with others, especially those in position of authority who had motives to get what they wanted.

I decided to lay it down for Brennan, "Here's the story. Every time we went to the bank, the first thing she'd do was put on that goddamn necklace. It was like it was part of her being. It was an act she needed to do to get through the day. It was also the only time she showed any kind of vulnerability. I think it made her feel real or relevant. Like there was a reason for her being alive. She must have felt when she wore it, that she was no longer an abandoned child. She always said she felt abandoned." I choked up a bit when I said those words out loud for the first time. If saying them was demoralizing, then living them had to be God awful. I instantly realized how Abby must have felt, living those words every day of her live, and how much emotional pain she endured just by not knowing her parent's identity.

I also told Brennan, "The first time I saw the necklace I was speechless. I guessed it was valuable, but I didn't know *how* valuable. I thought she looked like an Asian princess when she wore it, but I was in love, so my feeling for her enhanced her beauty.

"Yeah, DeLuca, *feelings and love* . . . make people do strange things, things they may never normally do, like lie, or keep things from people trying to help them."

"Abby would study the papers over, and over again, and I would look at her looking at them. Like I said, I was in love."

"Can you picture what she had on the top of the pile of papers that morning? Can you see what she was looking at? You saw it, you just didn't focus on it. Can you remember what she was doing while reviewing the papers?"

"That's a lot of *can yous* Brennan," I said as I leaned back into the cushion of the overstuffed couch and rested my head in its softness. Closing my eyes, I tried to recall the memories from the vault. I could see Abby. God, she is such a beautiful woman! Her long dark hair shone like silk while the gold chain against her pale skin appeared even more vibrant. When she leaned forward, the diamond's weight twirled it slowly just above the old linen paper she was reading. Her shirt pulled up above her waist and revealed her tattoo . . . Shit!"

"What is it DeLuca?" Brennan questioned immediately, not wanting me to lose that image.

"The tattoo."

"What are you talking about?"

"I don't remember seeing the tattoo! Usually when she stretched or moved a certain way, it would peek out from beneath her shirt." Events in the vault were still fuzzy and felt like missing footage in a movie. "I remember seeing the thief pawing at her, grabbing at her necklace, like it was a prize he needed to collect. She had said to him 'You won't take the necklace from me, it's mine now' odd . . ." It replayed in my head, like a record player needle hitting a scratch in the vinyl.

"Where are you, DeLuca?"

"In the vault, looking at Abby."

"Great! Now focus on the paper. What's on it?" Brennan repeated herself once more in a softer tone, "Paolo, what's on the paper Abby is looking at?"

I concentrated on the image. "It's a drawing with some Asian characters painted on it. It looks like one of those little trees."

"A Bonsai tree?"

"Yeah! Exactly! Except with characters where the leaves should be and a large character at the base of the tree. I think it was her family symbol or crest, an indication of her lineage. I think it was proof of who she was; I mean, *is.* But Abby never spoke Chinese, or could read it as far as I know."

"I think she knew a lot more than she let on, Paolo." Brennan donned a look of trepidation and squirmed in her seat.

"What's wrong Brennan?"

"Gut feeling, DeLuca. Always get them, and I always trust them. Abby knew something she hadn't shared with you, and I think this is way bigger than a coincidental bank robbery."

"At first, I thought you guys knew all about her past, since you were charged with her case. Guess I was wrong on that too."

"I'm telling you a lot more is afoot here than the agency knows about or more likely, is telling us. It wouldn't be the first time a government agency left its agents in the dark, or hung them out to dry." Brennan called loudly for Diego. "Boss, we've got a problem!"

I returned to the idea that I should not share any more information about Abby and me. These marshals, the two entrusted with my life, may be on the up and up, but then again, I got that gut feeling that has never steered me wrong. Something just doesn't feel right. Again. Two of the four federal officers feel out of place. Like they are hiding something deep inside they are afraid to reveal. The other two, well, I might be able to trust only one of them, and that trust is on the edge of a cliff ready to jump and end its life.

I'll give Brennan some leeway for now. Maybe she's not the hick she pretends to be, she wouldn't have made it this far into her career if she was. The gears in my head had been turning since we left Eden General. I need to start mentally preparing to find Abby and how to do it without getting either one of us killed. I'll let Diego and Brennan handle the formalities, but I'll take care of the details myself. That way, I'll know nothing is left to chance.

When Diego answered Brennan's shout, she summarized our conversation and described her on strong gut feeling. Diego saw the sternness in her posture. "Okay, so what do you want me to do?"

"I can call in a few favors, but I'll need a few more than I have. We must find out who else is following this case in the agency and in the FBI."

"I know better than to ask why. I guess we'll both be bankrupt in the favors department. If this is what you think it is, it may cost us both our jobs." After a moment, he continued, "I was going to retire anyway, might as well go out with a bang."

Seven

Sleep

Dinner was nothing more than pizza and beer. I excused myself from the marshals' company and challenged the long stairway to the second floor. Finding the first open room at the top of the stairs, which happened to be across from the room Brennan had chosen, I felt out of my environment and somewhat disoriented, the beer had something to do with that. Searching the dresser drawers and the closet, I found several pairs of pants, shirts, and a variety of shoes in different sizes. The clothes were close enough in size, and I was fortunate enough to find a pair of work boots among the dress shoes. They were well used but in good shape, and after trying them on, I felt a bit more comfortable.

After spending many days at Eden General in some type of coma, or whatever the doctors wanted to call it, the toll of the day had hit me harder than I had anticipated. Moving from the hospital, down six flights of stairs, and then through the parking garage to the car under my own power had drained any reserve energy I had, and all of the activity had brough back the pain from the surgery.

Reading the label on the pill bottle that Brennan had sweet talked a resident into supplying, I mumbled, "Oxycodone . . . should help me sleep. I took the oxy and a swig of PBR beer to wash it down, then I took one more for good measure. I needed to sleep. If I skipped out tonight after the marshals bedded down, I might make it to the end of the driveway. Going after Abby now, with no sleep and drugged up, with almost a six pack in me, I wasn't helping anyone. For the first time in years, I prayed, prayed that God would keep Abby alive until I could find her.

I sat on the bed and removed the sock slippers I had worn out of the hospital. Taking one more pill from the bottle, I washed it down with the fifth beer from the six pack from the kitchen fridge. Alcohol and pills are never a good thing, but today, I just didn't care. I wanted to sleep bad enough to do almost anything to get it. Without sleep, I was worthless to myself, and more importantly, to Abby.

My idea was to sleep and not dream. I needed a clear head tomorrow, so I could think straight- (note to self, not going to happen with booze and pills). Tomorrow, I needed to understand why the woman I love had lied about who she was. Well, maybe not lied; maybe she just didn't tell me everything she was going through because it always caused tension between us, or maybe she didn't have much more to tell. I was talking aloud in my alcohol-drug-induced stupor. I thought I heard the door open, or maybe someone closed it to give me some privacy. I really didn't care at this point.

I fell back onto the bed with my feet still on the floor, and sleep came fast, but it was far from restful. Okay, technically I passed out, but I still went to sleep. I had dreams of Abby, but not my Abby. It was some kind of subconscious message. In one dream, she was an Asian Princess. Servants encircled her, like a protective cocoon. Royal guards by the thousands stood between us, and each one I touched turned into a bonsai tree, their arms and legs turning into branches and roots. No matter how hard I tried,

I could not reach her, and that gave me a feeling of restlessness which interrupted any chance of a peaceful night's rest.

The theme was the same throughout the night, different scenes of the same movie with the same ending. No matter what I tried to do, Abby died each and every time. She would call out, "Paolo. Help me please. You know where to find me. Help me." Over and over and over. The scene repeated itself until I awoke early the next morning no more rested than when I had gone to sleep. Dead tired and over-medicated would not be helpful for me or Abby or to get me through the day. Maybe I shouldn't have had the last few beers. Yeah, let's go with that, one too many beers.

Hours later, I had to drag myself out of bed because I was dog tired and could sleep the day away if I wanted to. Stumbling into the bathroom, I found some shaving gear in the medicine cabinet above the double sinks and removed about two weeks' worth of beard. Gazing at myself in the mirror, I remember what Abby had always said after I shaved, "Handsome as ever, Paolo!"

After showering, I put on the scrubs again, checked the drive was still in my pocket, gathered up the clothes I had found in the room last night, and took them downstairs to find a laundry room. Doing this was more of a reason to explore the house than the need for clean clothes. I hoped either Diego or Brennan had left to get some food for breakfast. I was hungry for something solid and satisfying.

I got downstairs and saw that Diego was already up and gone, not that I knew for a fact that he had slept at all. Brennan stood on the other side of the counter, brewing a pot of damn-good-smelling coffee. Its aroma grew stronger the closer I got, and it captured most of my thoughts.

"Morning," I said as I passed the breakfast bar stools facing Brennan.

She returned the greeting with a nod.

I entered the room just off the kitchen and placed the clothes in the washer. The sound of the water flowing through the machine covered my opening the door to the garage. Just inside the door, and above the dryer were two key fobs hanging from a homemade hook. The four-bay garage housed a brand-new Toyota Prius, and some type of Mitsubishi electric car. My curiosity was piqued, because I had never seen one up close before.

I sat inside and read the dash, MiEV, I later learned that meant *Mitsubishi Electric Vehicle.* According to the chart on the sun visor, the car was supposed to get the equivalent of 112 miles per gallon. "I'll believe it when I see it." I said to no one. The car boasted its ability to run quietly, so when I was ready to go, I could get out of here without anyone hearing me leave. I softly closed the car door and went back inside smiling at the thought of the car.

I followed the smell of the freshly brewed coffee into the kitchen and I poured myself a mug full. I gathered the remnants of the day-old newspaper, and sat across from Brennan at the glass-top kitchen table. She wore just an oversized men's white dress shirt. Her legs were slightly parted, and her breasts were almost visible through the thin material of the shirt, and to me, just the right size. I must have been staring at her longer than I thought, I was startled when she spoke.

"Do you like what you see? Or are you just a closet pervert, DeLuca?"

I stammered some incoherent words and reddened from embarrassment. "I'm sorry, I didn't mean anything by it. I was just . . ."

"Fantasizing? What did you want to do? Do me right here on the kitchen table? Do you want me to jump up on the table top, or just bend over it?"

I didn't think I could get any redder than I already had, but I did.

She scanned her section of the paper and smiled, one like Abby used to do when she knew she had gotten the best of me. She laughed at my predicament, "Just busting your stones, DeLuca, but thank you for the compliment."

I tried to smile, but it was a weak effort and didn't work well. "Again, I'm sorry. Are you and Diego in some kind of relationship?"

"Ewww! No way, DeLuca!" she replied with a disgusted tone. "He's old enough to be my father! I found this shirt in the closet in my room, and it certainly isn't a Diego hand me down. I didn't bring any other clothes, short notice about a trip to Philadelphia and all. You know how it is, DeLuca, your boss calls and says get your ass to

Philadelphia, your flight leaves in one hour. I never got a chance to grab my Go Bag.”

“That explains the Dallas/Fort Worth Airport grocery bag you carried in last night,” I said to hopefully change the subject.

“Yeah, Got it at the airport news shop. Filled it full of magazines and junk food. Airplane food sucks, DeLuca.”

“I know that,” I said with some enthusiasm. “I’ve had some really bad meals on a few of my flights overseas. I want to apologize once more.”

She gave me that sly smile. She had me flummoxed, and she knew it, she liked being on top.

Diego entered with a Dunkin’ Donuts box and some sandwiches just in time to save me from further embarrassment. “Chow time!” He saw the smile on Brennan’s face, and what she was wearing, and he looked at me. “She caught you staring, didn’t she? Don’t worry DeLuca. You’re not the first. She did the same *do-me-on-the-thing* to me on our first assignment together. She gave me the *old-enough-to-be-her-father* line, and I was red for two days after that.

“Cause you guys are all the same!” Brennan laughed. “You get all wonky over any woman with a perky pair of boobs and an ass that looks good in a pair of jeans. Jeez, it’s just like being back in high school, except now I have a gun.”

We all got a laugh at the memory of days gone by. I genuinely like Brennan. I thought for a moment that if I had not met Abby and had somehow met Brennan, we may have hit it off. See, she was right.

"Day dreaming again Mr. DeLuca?" Brennan asked. "What would Abby say?"

I reddened all over again, not thinking it possible.

Diego laughed and tossed me a sandwich, hoping it would keep me from talking. He gave one to Brennan too as he sat at the table.

I lowered my head and stuffed my mouth full of egg and cheese so there was no more room for my foot. At least, that way I could stay out of trouble. Breakfast was good, it hit the spot. With some catsup and some hot sauce, it was even better.

Brennan excused herself and placed her cup in the sink and trash in the can under the sink. As she stood facing the sink, Diego whispered to me. "Don't do it."

She turned to leave the kitchen toward the stairs that led to the bedrooms. As she passed the table and reached the door to the next room, she said, "Stop staring at my ass DeLuca," in a tone I could not tell if she was playful or serious.

As I blushed red again, Diego laughed. "Can't say I didn't warn you!"

I finished breakfast in silence then put my plate in the sink. I removed the clothes from the washer in the laundry room and placed them in the dryer for a short tumble. I didn't think I was fooling anyone with housekeeping chores, but it made me feel better, pretending I was being stealthy.

Glancing over my shoulder to ensure Diego was not watching, I grabbed the Mitsubishi key fob from its hanger and entered the garage. I placed the fob in the cup holder since there was no key hole and looked for a way to start the car. Simultaneously depressing the brake pedal and touching the green start button on the dashboard, brought the vehicle to life. The gauges flexed all the way to the right and then settled into their designated places. There was no sound at all when the car started, "Silence is golden," I repeated from my Catholic school days. I pressed the button on top of the gear shift labeled "Stop" and the car shut down just as silently as it had started.

The pieces of my escape from the marshals were taking shape. With any luck, the rest would go just as easy. I scanned the garage for anything useful to aid my plan. There wasn't much, but I did find a Pennsylvania road map. I stuffed it into my waistband and headed toward the door into the house.

I left the key fob where I had found it and entered the kitchen through the laundry room. I poured a second cup of black coffee and sat at the table, perusing the Current Events section of the paper, and reading several articles. Thirty minutes later the dryer chimed three times, signaling the machine was finished with its assigned task.

While Brennan and Diego were in the family room on their cells, I turned on the television and put it on mute. Scanning the channels, I found nothing but daytime television shows filled with mindless content, no news updates on the robbery, or Abby for that matter.

Brennan was chatting with someone in Texas while Diego sounded like he was talking to some local field office. I watched them both, looking for any tell-tale signs of inappropriate behavior, but I didn't see or hear anything out of place. Then and there I decided to inform Brennan on all I knew about Abby and the contents of her deposit box. I decided to keep the flash drive secret for a bit longer, just until it was absolutely necessary to bring it into the light, then I'll let them know I have it.

Seeing the two marshals were still enthralled in their conversations, I checked out the rest of the first floor. The room three doors down from the family room was a home office. Tennis trophies lined the top of the bookshelves, and empty smiles came at me from the family photos on the wall above the desk. I sat at the desk and jiggled the mouse to boot up the computer. I opened the Google Chrome icon and launched some web page in a tab as a cover for what I was about to do.

Searching the desk, I found several drives like the one I had in my possession. I stuck one in the duck's mouth-shaped hole on the side of the computer. I erased the crap that was on it the inserted the drive from my pocket. When it booted, I immediately did a copy and paste file transfer. I secured the original drive inside my pocket. Opening the files on the drive revealed an Excel spread sheet with a column of names and several others with numbers next to the names, and then dates. I wasn't sure what they were, but I could guess.

Brennan called my name, so I quickly closed the file and removed the second drive. I slipped it into my pants pocket just as Brennan entered the room. I opened the Facebook tab with the other hand.

"What are you up to DeLuca?"

"I'm checking Abby's Facebook page. Maybe there are some clues as to who may be after her, or maybe something with the bank, I don't really know, just grasping at straws."

Brennan gave me that I-know-you-are-lying look, but played along anyway. "You wouldn't think she be desperate enough to post a picture of her necklace on her wall?"

I wasn't sure if that was a question or a statement. I scrolled down and found some well wishes for her safe return from her friends and some people I had met that night at the restaurant.

"Really not much here, Brennan. Maybe ten or twelve friends, most of them acquaintances, people she really didn't know."

"Anything derogatory posted on her wall?"

"Nothing. All positive stuff. Let me check her photos." I clicked the tab and about two dozen pictures appeared. Abby's wall was pretty much a dud. "Wait.

Here's a picture from the bank vault. I took this with my phone the first time she showed me the necklace." It was the only picture of the necklace anywhere on her page.

"I have this photo on my phone, and it should be on Abby's phone. I messaged it to her the day I took it. Abby was smiling when I took that picture. Her smile said, *I am content in my love for you.* It was my favorite picture of her.

"Why don't you give me her password, and I'll have my guys check it out? See if turn up anything."

"Really, Brennan. Like I don't know you guys looked at this stuff already. Come on, what do you take me for?"

Brennan looked at me in silence. She thought before she spoke. "Click on the pictures one more time, let's see what she posted."

"Great way to avoid answering a question Marshal, okay, here we go. Pictures of the Great Wall, some town in China, a Pagoda, cherry blossom trees. Oh yeah, those are from our trip to Washington D.C."

"Pretty!" Brennan said making conversation.

"Look here. Her settings are open to the public. Anyone can post here. Guess it was so she could get information from anyone who might have known her birth parents."

"Yeah, it's pretty much a dead end, DeLuca."

"Well, maybe someone with some knowledge of diamonds saw her picture and staged the robbery. I mean, it's possible."

"Yeah, someone wanted to steal a necklace that you insisted didn't exist. Not likely, DeLuca. I've been doing this job long enough to know when someone is spreading manure on my boots."

"I told you, Brennan, that I'd let you in and . . ."

"Don't get so defensive, DeLuca. I'm not talking about you. Something isn't right. My bullshit detector is going off, and it's making me crazy that I can't figure it out. Abby posts some crappy calendar photos and a picture of her wearing a diamond necklace, and that's supposed to set up motive for a bank robbery? Bullshit!"

Brennan was right. Something else was afoot under the surface of the bank robbery. There was more to it than the necklace. I knew all along the thumb drive was the target, and the necklace and Abby were bonuses for the crew.

Brennan was delving deeper into the questions for the motive behind the bank robbery. Her conversation was more out-loud thinking than it was conversing.

I shut down the computer and headed out of the office. Brennan followed me, punching an icon on her cell phone. As she spoke to someone at her office in Texas, I decided what to do. My intention was to talk with the marshals to see where we go from here. I had my own plan,

whether to include one, or both of them was still up in the
air. But, either way, I will find Abby.

8

Time Wasted

Diego headed to the FBI's Philadelphia office to see if he could do the cross-federal agency sharing information thing, but I never hold out for the sharing of information from one government agency to another. It's not in their nature to do so, and each agency has their own interests in mind no matter whose head is on the chopping block. I have never seen it in my experience with any branch of government, and I have no faith that Diego will get anything from the two FBI agents I'd met.

Those two government representatives, McGregor and Lee, didn't seem like the cooperative, sharing types. Agent McGregor was old enough to be Joe Friday's apprentice from his *Dragnet* days, and Agent Lee appeared to be the young, up and coming, new-wave rising star in the bureau. He emanated that go-ahead-and-fuck-with-me attitude, like he thought he was some kind of a bad-ass, or a "Very Special Agent" or some other name he gave himself. I had my suspicions about them, and no one other than me cared about what these two clowns were up to. Maybe Diego could get what he wanted from them, and if he did, any information is more than what we already know.

Diego had ordered Brennan to keep an eye on me while he went into the city, "Just to keep him safe," Diego had said.

I hadn't let either of them know about my background in the military, although Brennan suspected there was more to me than the calm surface waters showed.

She mentioned once how I was like a duck, calm movement on the surface while just underneath the surface all kinds of chaotic movements were happening.

I had been special ops when I'd served in the army, and Abby was the only person who knows the truth about my background. I didn't need anyone to keep me safe, I could handle myself, even in my weakened state. I had told Abby about the honorable medical discharge and why they had forced me to retire from the military. While down range, I had taken two rounds in the right thigh, and, as a result, I have two things to show for it, each one a trophy. The first was a nasty scar which, in the right light, looked like a praying mantis, and the second was a barely detectable limp. If it wasn't for my spotter, I would have bled out and died in the service of my country.

The damage to my muscle was sever enough that I could no longer hump a seventy-five-pound pack for any measurable distance, hence the discharge from the special forces unit I had loved so much. I could handle the limp and the scar, living with the medical discharge was something different. What I had a problem with the most was the death of the man who'd saved my life.

He had dragged my crippled ass through the thickest and hottest jungle in South America after miscalculations had compromised our op. He had thrown me into the waiting chopper at the rendezvous point and was standing on the lending strut when the round hit him in the back of the right arm, the arm he had been using to hold himself up with. The Chopper had taken off as he fell about one hundred feet to his death. I had screamed his name as I saw him hit the ground. The cartel was on him in seconds, and pumped three more rounds into him as he lay there. The shrink had tried to make me feel better by saying that he was probably already dead from the fall, but it was the brutality of the killing I still have nightmares about. The only thing that man has learned for waging war is the knowledge of how to kill each other more effectively.

Every now and then I raise a shot glass to him and say for all to hear, "Rest in peace MoJo. I owe you brother." Abby had asked me once, "If we ever have a baby, would you want to name our child after him?" I said I would, and then she asked, "Even if it's a girl?" Laughing, I would reply, "Especially if it's a girl!"

Once Diego was gone, I asked Brennan questions so I could figure out her mindset. We played tit for tat, asking each other questions about this and that, and I found out that she was an expert at the game. She gave only enough of an answer to force me to move on to the next question. It began with what's your background version of the game, where you originally from, what's your family history, did you always want to be a fed? I thought I knew enough about her now to judge that she played hard, but fair. She'll have your back, providing it doesn't compromise her career. I admire her for that. Fair, loyal, trusting, all you could ask for in a partner or a friend.

The women I have met throughout life all had one thing in common, they didn't make me feel inferior when I spoke with or worked with them. That's what I loved most about Abby, she was direct, and I knew where I stood with her. Brennan was the same way, except for her wit. If you called her a smartass, she would thank you for the compliment. Brennan wasn't a genius by numerical standards, but she was bright. Above all else, she was what intelligent people called *street smart,* something no law enforcement agency could teach. Also, she could sniff out things you had meant to keep hidden in the closet in your basement. I learned that with the necklace. I needed to be on my toes with her around, watching what I say and what I do or don't do.

I steered the discussion toward "the job" and why she was where she was. Brennan told me that most times her office assigned her to witness protection, it was the epitome of boredom. It usually entailed moving some government witness to a secure location until a trial started, or in some cases, setting them up in a new life in a new town with a new back-story, including a suitcase full of lies about where they hailed from.

"Can I ask you if you handled any major cases? Maybe a name I would recognize?"

Brennan smiled and glanced at the front door, maybe to see if Diego would reenter as she spilled some Texas marshal secrets. "You know I can't answer that DeLuca." And there was that smile again, the one that said, if I tell you, I'd have to kill you, but in a kind way.

It amazed me how two women like Abby and Brennan were so different, and yet shared some little identical quirks. It was quiet for some minutes before Brennan continued, "Those few instances when this job is not so boring, is what I live for. Those few seconds of unpredictable excitement or unexpected events, that short adrenaline rush makes it all worthwhile.

I probed a little deeper now that Brennan was opening up, and asked her for her impression of McGregor and Lee.

"I think McGregor is to old school to be concerned about. I could be wrong, it seems he's just going through the motions, just trying to make it to retirement."

"What about Lee?"

Brennan hesitated, maybe to choose her words wisely, "I don't trust him. I mean, I only met him for a few moments at the hospital after Mrs. Rubin read me the riot act, but I felt like he was hiding something. I'm thinking he has an agenda, like he's working a different angle along with the case. Like his loyalties lie elsewhere."

"You didn't tell me you met them. Did you tell Diego?"

"I did."

"And?"

"And nothing. They saw Mrs. Rubin talking to me, saw the badge around my neck, and then asked what I was doing there."

"What did you tell them?"

"I told them I was just leaving."

"Christ Brennan. Getting information from you is like trying to get water from a rock. Why are you making this so hard?"

"Because I'm a federal marshal, DeLuca. I can't just tell you everything you want to know. I took an oath, and that oath says I must protect you. If that means not telling you what I know, then you'll just have to deal with it." She paused to calm herself after her verbal eruption hit a six on the Richter scale.

I let the dust settle before I spoke again. "Sorry, Brennan. You're just doing your job. I didn't mean to push you so hard."

"Bullshit, DeLuca. You know you did. You got my Texas ire up to see how far you could push me."

"Yeah, I did. It won't happen again. So, I guess they returned to the hospital to arrest me?"

"I'm guessing they did."

Brennan and I stood in agreement about the FBI. We agreed to keep an eye on McGregor, but keep Lee in our sights, he's the one most likely to disappoint. If I need an ally through this thing with Abby, it'll be Brennan.

"I need to ask you something personal," I said.

"Personal or, *intimate* personal?" she asked with flirtation in her voice.

"More like belief personal. Have you ever experienced something like a physical connection?"

"You mean like talking to the dead stuff?"

"No, no, no. Not at all. More like a connection with a loved one, an alive loved one. Say, in a dream when someone is trying to tell you where they are by giving you a clue. Am I saying this clear enough?"

Brennan tapped one finger on the chair arm as if is she was thinking of how to answer without committing. "I believe we're all connected in some fashion, and I believe in a higher power, but then again, most of that shit is just hokey bull shit just to control the masses. Does that answer your question?"

"Did you really just use the word *Hokey* in a sentence?"

"I sure did, sugar!" she said in that sweet as sweet tea Texas drawl which she would let slip out sometimes. "Most people in Texas use it instead of a derogatory word. But the agency formally adopted it as the politically correct term for bullshit. Any more questions you need me to answer?"

"What's the deal with Diego?"

"He's a career man, got his thirty in last month and has the numbers to finally retire. Woo is his last assignment, and all he needed to do was field a phone call once a month until he signed his papers, which was going a whole lot better before Abby disappeared. The boss offered to send another agent in his stead, but Diego wanted to close out his tenure with a field assignment instead of sitting on the bench. Kind of going-out-with-a-bang theory."

"I'm not the sit-behind-the desk kind of guy myself."

Even after the friendly chat, I still wasn't comfortable with the situation at hand. I wasn't a prisoner, but I may as well have been. Brennan was on me like skin on a grape. I could feel her eyes on me, even if she was in another room. I couldn't do anything for Abby until I could ditch Brennan and Diego. I had to escape from the marshals' watchful eyes and their insistence that I stay in this opulent gilded bird cage. It was time to finalize the plan for my great escape and to get Abby.

"Don't get any ideas in your head, Paolo. I can read people pretty well. That's why I'm where I am, and that's what they pay me for. Understand?"

I didn't answer, but I did understand. She already knew I planned to get out of here as soon as they let their guard down. The only question remaining was when to go.

Nine

Escape

Getting off the couch after the conversation with Brennan proved difficult. Sitting still for so long had stiffened me up, and my limp was distinctly noticeable. Brennan asked if I was all right, and I lied to her that I was.

She spat, "You need to get some rest Paolo. You can barely walk."

"Resting won't help the limp, I'll be fine."

"You don't look like you'll be fine."

I turned around, "I said I'll be fine! Now back off!"

"I think you should be off your feet. When Diego returns, we'll see what he found out, and we can decide from there. Until then, park your ass somewhere and get comfortable."

"I appreciate your concern, Brennan, but I can handle myself. I'm tired of sitting around waiting for you guys to decide what the hell you're doing next. You and Diego can't do anything without directions from your office. Your hands are tied. Mine aren't. I'm going to find Abby."

Brennan stood and spoke like a lawman, "I cannot let you leave, Paolo."

I walked away from her, "You can't stop me, Brennan."

Before I reached the doorway that led to the kitchen, Brennan proved she could. She kicked me in the back of my knee on my bad leg, and I went down hard.

"Christ, Brennan, what the hell is your problem?"

She tried to help me up but I slapped away her hand. She knelt next to me and spoke in a soft, slow cadence, "You're my problem, DeLuca. You're stubborn, you're pig headed, and you're a big pain in my ass. Now, let me help you up.

I proved that I was stubborn and struggled to get to my feet, but I did manage to stand. "I'm going to get some rest." As I walked away from Brennan, I mumbled to myself, "Why do women always have to be right?"

"I asked you to do that earlier."

Reaching the top of the stairs was difficult, and, by the time I did, I was exhausted. After swallowing a few pain pills, I dozed off. When I woke because of the pain in my leg, it was four a.m. I dragged myself from bed, still wearing the clothes I wore yesterday, and carried my work boots, hoping for a soft, quiet walk in my socked feet past the room Brennan occupied. I touched my right pant pocket and felt the two flash drives within its cotton walls. I have learned from past experience that having a bargaining chip is a good thing but having a second bargaining chip at least guarantees you a onetime see-your-that-and-raise-you-this option.

I pushed the lever-style handle and pulled the door toward me. A slight screech from the hinges made me halt.

I listened for a response to the noise but none came. Opening the door to slip through, I stepped into the carpeted hallway and closed the door behind me. Walking past Brennan's room and noticing the door was ajar, I stopped and listened for any indication that she was awake and waiting to jump out to stop my escape from this opulent prison cell. Satisfied that she was sleeping, I descended the stairs into the living room. I guess it was his turn to stand night watch as I noticed Diego sleeping on the couch; good lord, can he snore—no chance of waking him up just by walking through the room.

With soft and deliberate movements, I crept closer to the coffee table, picked up Diego's cellphone and pocketed it. A gray-colored file folder stamped with the FBI logo lay on the table. Diego must have gotten it from our friends in the Philly office. I picked it up, tucked it under my arm and headed for the garage. I pulled the key fob from its hook in the laundry room, entered the garage and closed the door behind me. I sat on a bucket to pull on my boots; now I was ready to go.

The dull yellow moon light filtered by the opaque louvered roof window allowed me to move around the garage without turning on a light. I tugged the rope on the hinge that attached the garage door to the automatic opener. I placed my palms on the aluminum garage door and pushed it up as slow and quiet as it would allow. The steel wheels rumbled in their tracks; however, their sound reminded me of a bowling bowl rolling down an alley lane's gutter. At last, the door was full open, and I turned toward the glorified golf cart that would carry me away from Diego, Brennan, and a house worthy of a snobbish old man with even older money.

I opened the MiEV's door—the vehicle I chose to borrow—and squeezed inside. With two hands I pulled the door shut then dropped the fob into the gray cup holder next to the gear selector. Pressing the start button brought the car quietly to life as the gauges went to their maximum range and then returned to the idle position. Out of habit, I adjusted the rear-view mirror.

I nearly jumped form the car from the sudden shock of what I saw. In the car's tiny rear seat sat Marshal Brennan dressed in black with a hoodie concealing her blond hair.

"Christ, Brennan! You scared the shit out of me!"

"Going somewhere DeLuca?"

I reprimanded myself for not noticing her before I had gotten in the car. It reminded me of how rusty—or maybe the word should be *lax*—I have become since leaving the military. In the old days, that kind of misstep could get you killed, dead, real fast. And not only you, but your teammate as well.

Well, DeLuca. Which is it? Are you trying to sneak out, or are you just going out for an early morning meal?

I should have known Brennan would not have made leaving the house easy. Her presence reminded me of the assessment I had made of her earlier—she was smart and could be even in step with or ahead of who she was protecting. Either way, she was here, so she deserved my honesty.

"I'm going after Abby," I told her matter-of-factly and to the point—or maybe loud and clear is what I meant. Pick one, it wasn't a decision I would change no matter what she said.

"What makes you think you can help Abby anyway? You don't have a weapon, you can barely walk ten steps at a time, and, this getaway car, all you'll do is maybe sneak up on the kidnappers and either scare them to death or make them pee their pants from laughing so damn hard."

In her own smug way, Brennan had a point, but she still didn't know me as well as she thought. I did not want to play the tit-for-tat game. "I have a bargaining chip."

"Will you tell me what it is, or are we going to play twenty questions again, DeLuca?"

"No."

"No. No, what? No, you don't want to tell me, or no, we're not playing twenty questions?"

"No."

"All right, DeLuca. Have it your way."

I looked at her in the mirror, and she looked at me looking into her eyes. Time dragged as each of us waited for the other to say something as the *Jeopardy* theme song played in the background of my thoughts.

"What the hell are you waiting for, DeLuca? Back out the damn car before Diego wakes up and finds us in here like we just left senior prom for a quickie in Daddy's car." Brennan moved to the front seat as I shifted the car into reverse.

The electric motor whirred as I navigated the vehicle into the night air. I back into the roundabout that led to the main driveway which connected to the entry gates. The car sounded much louder than it really was, but everything seemed louder in the early morning hours.

"Nothing like driving a forty-five-thousand-dollar golf cart!" I said with sarcasm.

"Yeah, look at us. We're saving the fucking planet

During the drive I flipped through the file that Diego had gotten from the FBI. It contained typical investigative items—surveillance photos, official reports, hand written notes, one of which was a small yellow Post-it Note with a name and a phone number.

"Do you want me to look through that while you drive, Deluca? I mean, my life is on the line here," Brennan said with some concern.

"No, I'm good," I said as I ripped the Post-it from the photo and tossed the file on the back seat.

By daybreak we were at Fairgrounds Import facility just south of the airport. Pulling next to the box on the island in front of the rolling gate, I entered a six-digit code and pressed the star key. The gate inched open with a scream of its gears as the pulled the rusty chain. The noise also woke Brennan from a light sleep.

"Where the hell are we, DeLuca?" She stretched as much as she could inside the compact car.

I rolled through the gate. "I have to make a stop."

"At this fucking dump? What for?"

"Are you always this pleasant in the morning? Relax, Brennan. We're almost there."

Most of the complex was abandoned now, with the economy in the toilet. Not that the facility hadn't been heading that way anyhow, but the economy had just accelerated the process. A few other places here are occupied, and one was supposed to be a new night club, But the city council, in their wisdom, denied the license, so the nightclub's owner withdrew, and the property just continues to decay.

I headed north toward a remote area of the complex, which had housed foreign car imports. Remnants of greater days of glory littered the grounds with assorted car-body parts, tires, and an occasional empty car carrier perpetually awaiting its cargo. I pulled to the warehouse adorned with a large *77* painted on the ribbed aluminum, siding. The color of the numbers had long since faded to an almost invisible gray, but they could still be read. They stand as a testament to a once great and prosperous time in the city's history.

"This is where you have to make a stop?" Brennan asked. "Do you have some pet rats to feed or something?"

I told Brennan to move to the driver's seat as I got out. After opening the combination lock, I went through the man door and entered the building. I hit a button on the wall, and the two large doors opened wide enough to get the little car inside. Once Brennan drove in, I hit the button again, and the doors closed, plunging us into darkness. I threw the red-tipped lever on the breaker box, and the lights came on as they warmed with the current. Brennan exited the car and started asking rapid-fire questions.

"If you wait a sec, I'll show you why we're here." I went to one of the two SEA-BOX storage containers. They were a reminder and a link to a former life. As I punched in a code on the key pad, Brennan just couldn't remain quiet any longer.

"DeLuca, I don't think you've been completely honest with me. Who the hell are you, and what are we doing here?" The corners of her mouth curled a bit as she tried not to smile.

I looked at her. "Follow me, if you want to see some really cool shit!"

I pushed the switch inside the door, and the SEA-BOX came to life. The overhead lights came on, and two computer screens flashed blue as the drives booted up. Several weapons racks hung on the wall opposite the computers.

Brennan whistled as she beheld it all. "What are you? Some kind of spook, DeLuca? You got enough shit here, illegal shit I might add, to outfit a small army. Christ, how the hell did you pay for all this?"

"Thanks to my father, money was never an issue."

"What's your dad do for a living?"

"He's dead—has been since my second year of service I missed his funeral because I was down range—couldn't make it home."

"Sorry, DeLuca."

"Don't be. He and I were good . . . but mom—she's another story."

"Sorry—"

"Enough reminiscing. Sit there, Jane." I pointed to an overturned wooden crate.

"Jane? So now we're on a first name basis, DeLuca?"

"Do you want to hear this or not, Brennan?"

She raised both hands in mock protest as she sat at one of the two terminals. I briefed her on my past life as an Army Ranger and Black Ops Specialist. After I was done, she said Diego had done a background check on me, and nothing like this came up. All Diego found was your discharge from S1 and something about being a paper pusher in the army. "I'm guessing now that it was all bullshit."

"That's the standard army-issue story for operators when the detach from service. Now, here's the thing, Brennan. We've wasted enough time. I'm going full op mode to get Abby back. If you want out, just say the word. I'll go it alone."

"A girl's got to have a little fun every now and then, DeLuca. I'm in. If anything happens to you, I'm still in a jam, so we're partners in crime from now on." She spit in her hand and extended it for me to shake.

I declined.

"Okay, you're in, Brennan. What has stuck with me the most from the army was to always be prepared, no matter the situation. That's why the SEA BOX's, are loaded with what they're loaded with. Make sure you grab that black duffel bag back by your feet on the way out, because we're not coming back for anything."

"Got it. What's inside?"

"You know . . . cash is king! Now get your ass on that keyboard and find this Taine guy. See if you can track his phone number." I gave Brennan the slip of paper I had taken from Diego's FBI file.

"I can think of better things I'd like to get my ass on," Brennan said as she smiled.

I rolled my eyes and told her to stop with the double-entendre stuff and that we didn't have time to fuck around.

"There's always time to fuck around, DeLuca."

"Find out if that's a GPS-capable cell and get me a location. And for Christ's sake Brennan, keep it in your pants. I'll gear up the car."

Brennan smiled, because she knew that she had me randied with all the flirting. It was her way of keeping control of a situation when she had none. She spoke as I left the SEA BOX. Yeah, great, a geared-up golf cart. That'll scare them."

"Not *that* car. Find me the location of the phone that goes with that number."

"Where did you get this--? Never mind. It's probably better if I didn't know."

After opening the other SEA BOX, I started the red and black 1970 Dodge Charger—a great muscle car. I parked the MiEV inside and secured the box again.

Brennan was still on the computer, waiting for information on the cell's location and, at the same time, Googling Taine.

I loaded the trunk with guns and ammo and enough hardware for a street gang, hoping it should keep us safe while we looked for Abby. By the time I was done, Brennan had finished with her search. We shut down the first SEA BOX and locked the doors. I punched in a long string of digits and hit the pound sign. The keypad toned three times and flashed red. I did the same with the pad on the other box.

"Nice ride," Brennan exclaimed. As she threw the black duffel into the Charger's trunk.

"It'll do. Let's move. We don't have much time."

"Why? What the hell did you just do?" When I didn't answer, she said, "DeLuca! What the hell?"

"No worries, Brennan. I just put the boxes on lock down, just in case. Now, get in." I handed her one of my two Glocks. "For insurance. Did you track down Taine's location?"

"Yeah, and it's her location."

I regarded Brennan with surprise, "*Her*?"

"Yeah, her. And it's just Taine, no last name. Just like those old bitches, Cher and Madonna. I couldn't find much about her on the internet. Taine owns a property in Chinatown. Want to bet it's a front for something else?"

"Not this time. I've lost enough lately."

"Can I ask you something personal?"

I knew sooner or later she would pry. It was in her nature to not let anything go; she just had to peek under another rock to see what she could find.

"Oh, God. Here we go."

"Lighten up, DeLuca. I'm just asking for a little background here. It's nothing big."

"What?" I said annoyed.

"Does Abby know about your past—the military stuff? Or is it still a secret you keep locked in the pantry in your kitchen?"

"Abby knows everything. I held nothing back. Even if she thought it was too descriptive, I told her about it."

"How'd she take it?"

"She made me promise never to do anything like that again. Or, in this case, I promised never to do what we're about to do."

"Will that promise make this hard for you?"

I looked Brennan in her eyes. "No, I'm sure Abby will forgive me."

Brennan turned away, "didn't you say we didn't have much time?"

I started the car, hit the gas pedal a few times then put it in gear. The engine roared with some old-fashion, Detroit muscle-car power as the dual mufflers vibrated the seats.

Brennan grinned as she spoke above the engine's roar. "This car can make a girl hot."

I shook my head. "You just can't help yourself, can you."

I pulled out of the warehouse and hit a button on the console just above the rear-view mirror. The warehouse doors shut behind us as I drove away.

Brennan looked over her shoulder. "Just fucking amazing, Batman. Is that a factory option or something you whipped up in your bat cave?"

I just starred at her.

"Okay, I know. You put the warehouse on lock down, just in case, blah, blah, blah."

"Where we headed?" I asked, purposely avoiding her sarcasm as I drove toward the exit gate.

"Middle of the city, head to Chinatown. Whoda thunk that?"

"You mean, Center City?"

"Same-same, DeLuca."

"Chinatown it is!"

Going heavy on the gas pedal, we arrived in twenty minutes easy. I pulled into a structure that had once been a vacant building. It was now a multi-level Park Here place courtesy of the city's revitalization project. They rezoned this area, eliminated the drug problems the old tenement house offered its residents. Emanate Domain was now a more-than-useful tool for the city fathers to take what someone else owned—for example, the Cooper Park Project. The mayor blamed his opponent for everything that happened with the project and won his reelection in a landslide.

If you paid cash, the parking fee was twenty dollars, which usually ended up in the attendant's pocket. I gave him a fifty and told him to keep the change if he could get me a spot close to the exit.

Brennan and I walked to the stairwell door, which exited to the street. She was still bitching about having to listen to a sports talk station on the radio during the drive.

We had our own Dallas-versus-Philly conversation in the car, and it came with an offer to a game in the new Dallas stadium. I said I would put it on the maybe column of bucket list.

"Nah, I mean it DeLuca. Come to Texas, and see a game with me. I'll even wear my short-cut Aikman jersey, just for you."

Brennan definitely enjoyed flirting; I needed to ensure this flirtation didn't blossom into anything close to what Brennan was hinting at.

"If I had known you were a Dallas fan, I would have made you walk here,"

Brennan smirked and rolled her eyes.

"What's the address we're looking for?"

"Nine-thirty-four. It should be ahead on the left."

Walking toward our destination, I checked the numbers above the building's front door. "You sure this is it, Brennan? Did you double check the address?"

"I know how to do my job, DeLuca. I made a list and checked it twice. This is the place. It's not what I expected, but the address is correct. Let's go in and see what the hell we can find."

We crossed the street and entered the New Lin Chong Wu Grocery store. I scanned the store for anything out of the ordinary. Things looked okay, but looks can be deceiving. A rear door was propped open with an upturned fruit crate, which can be an exit to a back alley and another way out if things got ugly.

The woman at the counter spoke with a heavy Asian accent. "Can I help you?" It was more of a *help* with an *ar* sound then an *el* sound.

Brennan displayed her badge. "United States Marshal Brennan—here on special assignment. I'm looking for a woman named Taine."

Shit, shit, shit, shit, shit . . . I exhaled in frustration; this was not the plan.

Brennan regarded me as if I was again judging her professionalism, which I wasn't. This is not the way I would have made the introductions; I would have begun with some pleasantries, like *good morning* or *nice day today.*

With Brennan flashing her badge and the tone of her voice, the woman behind the counter forgot how to speak English. She ranted in Chinese at the pace of a sprint runner in a hundred-yard dash. Finally, in broken English, she said, "You go now! Nothing here for you!"

Brennan began to protest, so I grabbed her arm and pulled her outside.

"What the fuck are you doing, DeLuca?"

"Christ, Brennan. You just fucked things up. People down here see a badge, and it's all over. Nobody will talk to us now. Damn you, Brennan."

Her face reddened with anger.

When she started to rebut, I gave her more. "We need to do things differently. No badges. No official law enforcement ID. Nothing that says you're official *anything,* or we'll never find Abby. Got it?"

Brennan didn't answer, she just stayed angry, biting her lip to the point of drawing blood.

"If you don't do this my way, you're gone. I'll do this on my own, which I probably should be doing anyway."

"Okay. Sorry if I fucked up in there, but let me set you straight. We'll do this your way, but, if it gets ugly in there, I won't hesitate to end it, no matter what you say."

That was the Brennan that got her to where she is today—willing to compromise but willing to step in and take the lead when she thought it was necessary.

I waited and counted to ten to think about her statement. "Okay, we'll go with that as long as you do what I say when I say. Now, do me a favor, wait in the car and calm your ass down."

I tossed her the keys and headed back inside to talk to the old woman. As soon as I entered, she yelled again. I raised my hands in mock surrender, and she quieted down.

"My name's Paul Lunk. I'm here to see a woman named Taine."

The old woman studied me, like she was dissecting my soul, before she replied in that heavy accented voice, "Why?"

"I need her help."

"For what?"

"I'll tell her when I meet her."

The old woman thought for what seemed like an hour before she spoke. "She not here now. You come back later."

"When?"

"Later!"

I had no choice but to agree and turned to leave.

She spoke to my back as I reached the door. "You leave license or no come back."

"Why?"

"Because I say so."

I faced her, and, since she held all the cards, I handed her my fake ID.

She ripped it from my hand and looked at the photo and then at me, scrutinizing the document, like she was a border agent. "When you come back, don't bring policewoman or no meet Taine."

"Yeah, I'll come back later."

"You come back tomorrow."

"Why tomorrow?"

"Tomorrow." She nodded toward the door.

Things had improved some without Brennan at my side. At least I had gained the smallest bit of trust with the old woman and had worked my way in to see Taine. The fake license I had left would withstand deep scrutiny, if pressed to see if I was who I said I was. It was always good to have another identity when trying to infiltrate a closed community. These people would have trusted me if I had been with Abby, but two Caucasians in Chinatown asking for someone specific would definitely present trust issues.

I met Brennan at the car park and briefed her on the events in the grocery store. I could tell she was still upset with my outburst toward her.

"So, what do we do until tomorrow?" she asked.

"We visit the locals and find out if the police know anything about the robbery suspects."

"Okay, but I'm driving."

Brennan smoked the tires leaving the parking garage. The pedestrians crossing at the corner scattered as she turned left through the intersection. Good thing no cops were around, or she may have four tickets by now, and we barely had traveled two-hundred yards. Twelve minutes later, we were at the local sixth police district headquarters at 235 North Eleventh Street, which was only a mile from the parking garage.

"I think we could have walked here faster," I told Brennan.

She grinned. "Maybe so, but you would have missed all the fun of my driving here."

"Let's go inside. Maybe the desk sergeant can direct us to whomever is handling the case. We're only four or five blocks from Franklin Bank. Since this scenario is badge appropriate, Brennan, you take the lead."

"Roger that, DeLuca."

Once inside she was all federal marshal, ready to use her best Texas accent to charm her way into the innermost regions of the building. She walked with an authoritative swagger to the desk and announced us. Showing her credentials, she spoke just loud enough for the sergeant to hear. "I'm United States Marshal Jane Brennan, and this is my partner, Marshal Diego." She nodded to the left, indicating me. "We'd like to speak to whomever is investigating the Franklin Bank robbery." She did not use any polite verbiage; it was strictly by-the-book-law-enforcement formalities.

The desk sergeant instructed a patrolman to escort us to Detective Richard's office. "I'll call up and let him know you're coming. And could you tell him that he still owes me twenty for the game?"

Brenna told the sergeant that she would relay the message.

We followed the rookie to the second floor. The kid looked like he was sixteen—acne and all.

"God, they are making them young these days," Brennan teased. "I bet he doesn't even have one bullet in his service weapon."

We arrived at CID, which a large blue sign with white letters clearly announced. The rookie made introductions then scurried off like a rat in a maze to complete his other mundane duties, such as getting Detective Richard's an iced coffee from across the street.

"And don't forget the sugar this time!" Richards yelled after him. "Damn rook, don't remember to load his weapon if I don't remind him. His training office is out with the flu, so I get to babysit until he returns. Now, what is it I can do for the US Marshal Service?"

Ten

Local Leos

Detective Michael Richards was not what I had expected of a local cop; he had no discernable Philadelphian accent when he spoke. His attire was completely professional—his shirt well pressed and his tie pinned in place to keep it out of his way. The only flaws in his appearance were his rolled-up shirt sleeves and his apparent love of cheesesteaks. Their wrappers littered the top of his desk and overflowed the trash bin. A football team coffee mug half fill of cigarette butts sat on the top of a stack of case files resting on the in box. He saw me scrutinize the desk and took a mental note of it.

He gawked at Brennan again.

I almost warned him, but I wanted to be on the other side of her belittlement for once, just to see what it felt like.

He stared a moment to long admiring her, then Brennan hit him with the do-me-on-the-desk line. Diego was right. It was funny when someone else was getting the brunt of Brennan's smart-ass attitude, mostly because the recipient totally unexpected it.

Richards just shook his head, thinking better of replying. He asked again what he had asked before but with a bit more annoyance. "How can I help you?"

"We're working the Franklin Bank robbery, following a lead on a string of robberies that originated in Texas." A little white lie, no harm done.

"Yes, I pulled that case. These guys are not your guys. I really can't help you two. The FBI took over the case, something about a kidnapping of a local resident. Maybe you should talk to them."

Instinctively, Brennan went into her sweet little ole Texas accent. "Darlin, we already talked with the FBI, and they are pretty much useless. They really didn't want to share anything with us. I was hoping ya'll could help us out a little." She must have been getting her way with this ploy for years, and it seemed to be working now.

Richards surveyed us one more time, again assessing Brennan and I trying to determine if we were for real. "Okay, here's the lowdown. Missing Asian woman, twenty-four years of age, and a missing antique diamond necklace worth almost five-million dollars, taken along with the woman. Only one other safety deposit box was opened, but they didn't take anything from it. The company that rents the box swears that they had not yet placed anything in it—or so they claim. We have suspects with Russian-made weapons and controlled explosions that killed four tellers on detonation. They then executed the remaining employees along with the customers." He looked at me. "Then they shot the manager in the head after she had cooperated with the suspects, and, to round it up, an unknown accomplice executed her two children in their home." Richards eyed both of us. "Now, what's that spell out to you two?" He waited a few moments again, not expecting an answer. "Something don't smell right! That's a lot of fire power for a damn jewelry heist!"

"And you think there's more to it?" Brennan asked.

"Hell yeah! I'm wondering what was in the other opened box! Listen, I may be a local cop, but with the bank's lawyers saying, "Whatever the customer states, is good enough for us,' and with the company insisting nothing was in the box, I think it all smells like a big pile of fresh dogshit!"

"Ya sure that's not the cheesesteaks, darlin?" Brennan asked, mocking his attitude.

"Yes, I'm sure! Something isn't right with this story. Banks don't normally keep a record of what's inside someone's deposit box, so why did the manager have a list of all the boxes' content in the vault? You two look like country mice lost in the big city, so I'll give you a leg up on this case. The FBI will not investigate any further into Computer Logic, the owners of the second box. Why? I have no damn idea. My source at the bank said he was with the company's representative when he needed access to the box."

"And you think that's when they placed something in the box?" Brennan asked.

"Probably! And why request access to a box you know you have nothing in? And get this, to top it off, guess who runs and maintains the computer systems for Franklin Bank. Yeah, that's right, Computer friggin Logic! Here's my scenario, Marshals. I think a company rep came to the bank one bright and sunny day, put something in the deposit box and then the bank' information technologies manager wiped the vault visitors log to hide any activity associated with it."

Brennan tapped a finger to her bottom lip. "I guess it's plausible. Ms. Stone could have instructed the IT guy to delete the log entry. I'm curious though, how reliable is your source at the bank?"

Richards looked annoyed at the thought of Brennan even slightly disrespecting his informant. "If he told me the president of the United States was a Russian citizen, I would not give it a second thought."

"What do you think the rep put in the box?"

"Don't know. Don't fucking care."

"And you expect me to believe a computer logic employee placed something into the company's deposit box, and then the same company hired a bunch of thugs to rob the bank to retrieve their own property? Seems a bit farfetched, Richards."

"I said it was my scenario, I didn't say that's how it went down."

"But you're running with it as your number-one investigation."

"Not officially. Remember, FBI took the case."

"What *is* your official stance?"

"Jewel heist, just like the FBI thinks it should be."

Brennan exhaled loudly. "Got anything else to share before we go, Detective?"

"You know everything I know."

She eyed Richards once more before we left his office, maybe gauging him on his loyalty to his source at the bank. "Well, Detective, thanks for all your help, this being our first time in the big city and all."

Richards waited until we were almost through his door before shouting at our backs, just to prove we were treading on his turf. "One more thing, Miss Country Mouse."

We turned to look at him.

"I have documentation that says Miss Abhijishya Woo may not be who she claims to be."

Those words hit me hard—a reminder that Abby could have been misleading me all this time. I pushed the thought from my mind.

Brennan's interest piqued enough for her to approach his desk. "And will you share that documentation with us, Detective?"

Richards rolled his eyes at her attempt to play the country bumpkin roll again. "Yeah, but not here. Give me the address where you're staying, and I'll have someone drop off a copy of my report. Too many eyes around here to see me giving you anything. Things get around, you know."

Brennan gave Richards the address. And we left the station. "You think he's sending it to the safe house to give him time to check us out?" I asked her.

"No doubt. But like he said, things get around. I think the meeting went well."

Minus the bit about Abby possibly not being Abby, I thought he was holding back, not giving us anything more than he needed to. I asked her if she had any gut feelings about Richards or noticed anything abnormal about him or his office. Again, I was testing her powers of deduction and observation; it was just a habit.

She said no, so I pointed out the military tattoos on his forearms. "I've seen those tats before. Richards has operator experience. He must be ex-military. Did you notice how he sized us up as soon as we entered the office? I'm betting he was special forces. One thing for sure, he's got you pegged for being smarter than that Texas sass says you are."

"You got all that from one short visit to his office?"

"That, and the fact a picture of him and five other military guys hung on his office wall. I'm sure I know one of the guys in the picture. I was down range with him in Paraguay."

Brennan smirked. "Paraguay? You want to fill me in on that operation, DeLuca?"

I retorted the adage, "I can, but then I have to kill you."

Brennan laughed at the thought of me besting her and gave me that coy smile of hers. "I'm driving home darlin."

"You're going home, Brennan. I've got one call to make, and then I'm going off the grid. I pulled Diego's cellphone from my pocket and searched the contacts list. Finding what I needed, I hit the call icon.

"What are you doing?"

I just looked at her as Agent McGregor answered the call. "How can I help you, Marshal?"

I spoke into the phone softly, almost pleading. "Listen, I kind of screwed up. I lost the file you gave me. My boss is on my ass to close this case." I hesitated to give the deception some tone of reality. "Look, McGregor. I need your help, agent to agent. I need another copy of the file. Don't make me beg. The phone was silent. "If I don't get this case closed soon, I'll have to retire on their terms, McGregor, not mine."

"Alright, but you owe me. Where do you want it sent?"

"Have Lee drop it off at the sixth district police station. Tell him to give it to the desk sergeant. I need to pay an official visit there anyway." I gave him the address and thanked him again. He disconnected before I could finish. I handed Brennan the phone. "Tell Diego I apologize for taking his phone."

Brennan raised one eyebrow as she took the phone. "I guess it's better if I don't know your plan, DeLuca. So how do I reach you if I need to?"

"If I find anything new, I'll contact you."

"Don't you trust me, Paolo?"

"It's not a question of trust, Brennan. If this is what I think it might be, I don't want you getting hurt. I couldn't live with myself if something happened to you while trying to get Abby."

"I can handle myself. And please call me *Jane*. I like hearing you say my name."

I pictured a thousand scenarios of hooking up with Brennan, and none of them could happen. I love Abby, and nothing will change that, including Brennan, so I compromised. "Okay, Jane. But that's as far as it can go. I can't have feelings for you because of Abby, and all you can do now is just cloud my judgement."

Brennan smiled and began to turn away. "I'll take that as a compliment . . . again, DeLuca. But know that I care for you, and, if there is any chance, just say the word." Brennan hugged me, kissed me on the check and whispered in my ear, "I'll be waiting."

Back at the parking garage, I took the duffel from the trunk, stuffed a few more weapons in it and closed the lid. I gave the key to Brennan. She entered the car without saying a word and left me in a plume of smoke as she burned rubber off the tires. I stared after her as she sped down the street, making pedestrians jump back onto the sidewalk. I smirked as I headed toward the café across from the police station.

I sat at an outside table and ordered a coffee from the redheaded waitress wearing way-to-tight yoga pants.

The duffel bag rested between my feet just within reach. It contained the few things I would need to get Abby out of danger—weapons, cash, a few assorted explosive devices, and some other mundane things. I spotted Lee approaching the station house.

As the waitress brought me the coffee, she asked for payment.

I paid for the coffee, and gave her an extra fifty and told her she could keep it if she held my bag for me until I was done at the police station.

She agreed.

As Lee got closer to the station, it seemed like anyone who was Asian would cross the street to avoid him. I thought it was odd, since he was well dressed, and I knew that he was FBI. But I still have my doubts about him, and this scene may confirm my suspicions of who he really was.

Lee entered with a manila envelope under his arm, and moments later he came out without it.

I watched him leave, and as soon as he was out of sight, I headed across the street. Reentering the station, I asked the desk sergeant if I could see Richards.

He spoke at me more than to me, never looking up from the newspaper. "Richards told me that if you came back, I should send you right up, Marshal."

I looked at him a bit amused that he thought I was really Brennan's partner.

"You know the way." He pointed to the stairs.

I walked toward them, and he called out, "Hey, Diego, you forgot this!"

Heading back and then taking the envelope, I thanked him for his help. As I climbed the stairs toward Richard's office, I took one of the two thumb drives from my pocket and put it in the envelope. Once in his office, I sat in the chair next to his desk., just like I was a perp. Truth is, I soon would be.

"I'll be with you in a sec." Richards said as he turned his chair's back to me, so I could not hear any of his conversation. I took advantage of the situation and placed the envelope under the coffee cup holding down his in box.

When he completed his call, he turned back to me and got right to it. "What unit?"

"Eighth Special Forces Group out of Fort Gulick, Panama. Worked S1 out of A-company. How about you, Detective?"

"I was an instructor at the Kennedy Special Warfare Center out of Fort Carson, Colorado. Did you have Rizzo at ranger assessment? And it's *Michael*"

"No, Rizzo was gone when I went through. I had Spunkmeyer. He was a real prick. He DOR'd eleven guys between the bus and the barracks."

He laughed aloud in in some long-ago memory of his training.

"I recognized Kirkman in the photo on your wall. He's a damn good operator."

Richards saddened. "*Was* a good operator. Took a bullet in Iraq, bled out trying to rescue three team members. He got them out but didn't last the trip back to base camp. Kirk was a real hero, not like these lard asses around here!" He took a deep breath. "What can I do for you, Marshal?"

"Let's be straight. I'm not a marshal; I'm Abby's fiancé—just so we're truthful."

Richards banged his fist on the desk then pointed at me. "Damn! I knew I've seen you before. You're the guy on video, you're thee Paolo DeLuca."

"Guilty as charged," I said.

"You're the Paolo DeLuca who was in the vault at the time of the robbery, and that makes this shit very complicated."

"Yeah, it does. And I respect your position in this. What do you have saying Abby isn't Abby."

Richards took time contemplating his next step. The department frowned upon sharing sensitive case information outside of the district, and sharing it with a civilian—especially one tied to the case itself—could be disastrous for his career. "I'm only doing this because the FBI is known for screwing up this kind of case, so maybe I can do it for them." Richards opened his top desk drawer and removed a file folder with SENSITIVE stamped in red with thick, bold lettering.

He asked me how long I've known Abby, and I told him I've known her less than a year.

He handed me the file. "I have a contact in the CBP."

I opened it and found that it held a photocopied piece of paper. "That is a copy of a passport document for a passenger on an international flight inbound from China almost fourteen months ago, before you met her."

"And . . .?"

"She was held at customs in Philly International. Her passport didn't hold up to scrutiny after the agent felt something was off with this version of Abby Woo."

"Like what? It looks real to me."

"CBP said she looked rattled, almost scared. Then he said when he looked back and forth between her and the passport photo, she started perspiring. They held her at airport security until they cleared her several hours later."

"What's wrong with it?"

"Port of origin is off. She said she had arrived from one location, while her paperwork said she came in from another. Usually that kind of thing goes unnoticed. State police kept her in a holding cell until the Chinese Embassy got involved, claiming some bullshit diplomatic immunity. They said she was the daughter of one of the Chinese ambassadors, and CBP had to release her. So, here we are a year later, and this same woman in this passport photo gets kidnapped during a bank heist in Philadelphia. Like I said, smells like dogshit."

I regarded Richards with great frustration. "Listen, Detective, although I've known her for what may be considered only a short time, I know Abby. And the woman in this photo—she is not my Abby!" Something is different about this woman. I can't put my finger on it, but I know for a fact"—I held the paper in one hand and tapped at it with the forefinger of my other hand— "this is not Abby!"

"What's different? And what happened the night before the robbery?"

I had to think hard about the night before the robbery. Recent events made things hard to recall. "She had a concert performance the night before they took her from the vault. I stayed home that night. Normally, I would see her perform, but we had fought earlier, so she was upset and told me to stay home, and I did as she asked."

"Anything else?"

"I woke that morning, and Abby was already awake. She said she came in late and slept on the couch, that she didn't want to wake me. Shit! I should have known something was amiss!"

"Like?"

"Abby never slept on the couch. If we fought, I would be the one in the doghouse—it was her house, her rules. I should have picked up on the little things. Damn it! I just wasn't paying attention! Now that I'm thinking about it, she asked me that morning where we kept the sugar. She would never use sugar in her coffee, always Sweet and Low. God, I'm getting sloppy in my old age."

"Maybe . . . or maybe it has something to do with the way you feel about her. Love can cloud your mind; make you see things everyone else can't. Let me ask you this, what are the chances of two Asian women looking that much alike and both being concert violinists?"

"Pretty . . . much . . . zero."

"Pretty much zero. That's why the case is out of my hands. Because of the FBI, I can't do anything *officially*. What's your next move?"

"I'm finding Abby, my Abby. Then I'm finding their Abby and giving her an Academy Award for best performance in a Bank Vault, which will be accompanied with some repercussions.

Richards wrote a number on the back of his business card then handed it to me. "That number is a burn phone. It's untraceable. Call me just before things go down, and I'll come help you—off the record of course."

"Of course."

"As an officer of the law, I must tell you that I will consider any actions you take against this woman as an assault and premeditated, and I will hold you accountable to the fullest extent of the law. Am I clear, DeLuca?"

"Rest assured, Detective, I have no plans on hurting anyone," I said almost convincingly.

We shook hands, and I left. Soon he would find the file I had left on his inbox, along with the flash drive. If I know him like I think I do, he'll make good use of that information.

Eleven

Brennan

Watching Brennan work, watching her interact with other law enforcement officers and watching her talk with persons of interest, all led me to one conclusion; she loved her job. She loved it as much as I had loved being down range when I was in the military. Maybe *loved* is not the best word for doing what I did—maybe it was because I believed that what I did mattered, and it gave me satisfaction and a feeling of making a difference. The best part of being special forces was being operative—the actual act of *doing* in doing is what mattered.

The talk I had with Brennan revealed a lot about her, even though she kept a door locked and allowed no one through. She was smart—not as smart as Abby but intelligent in a different way. I'm willing to bet Brennan has something like an eidetic memory, more commonly known as a photographic memory. She never took notes during any interview, interaction, or conversation, yet her ability of total recall of every detail of a conversation was impressive.

Like me, she didn't fall for any of the shit the FBI was spewing, and she had a unique way of looking at things related to the case she was working on. She quantified them in relation to the job alone, disconnected and without emotion. Most officers carried something from each case to the next one, and it either clouded their judgement, making them complacent, or incited an emotional outburst, causing either removal from the case or a reprimand or both. Her ability to separate herself from her interviewees' negative energies and their emotions resembled how surgeons dealt with a patient's death. It was a distant, cold, almost non-human emotionless ability that made her good at her job.

I don't see the banter between us as sexual; I see it as flirtatious. As I had thought, Brennan had been getting her way with that flirtatious, sexy Texas accent for many years. She said it begun in junior high school when boys started noticing her, and she used it to take advantage of their hopeful generosity. They had an ulterior motive, and so did she.

Brennan also told me that in college, she used it to influence fellow students as well as her professors. Flirting with her peers had placed her at the top of what was known at the college as The Hunt. It was a simulated activity in which she and the other students attempted to solve a faculty member's murder. Although students accomplished The Hunt during a twenty-four-hour period—beginning the day before the college's founding celebration and ending with the last chime of the six-p.m. campus clocktower bell the day of—Brennan had it solved by noon on the day of the festival. She had accused the Dean—the head of the criminal justice department-in the death of his assistant. She postulated that Dean Johnson had murdered Professor Simons because of his popularity and because he was next in line to take the position of Dean. He then attempted to blame it on a coed who Simons was having an affair with; Brennan's prize for solving the murder was an additional four course credits and an exemption from final examinations for all criminal justice related classes.

After the state police had accepted her into the academy and she achieved the graduate with honors tag, the US Federal Marshal Service recruited her. She was still using her talents to get what she needed from her peers and those she protected or arrested. Brennan also told me that she had declined two promotions to remain in her current position. One more refusal and her career would be over; she would be relegated to desk duty until retirement. Passing on a promotion was rare, especially for a female; passing on two was unheard of.

I'm sure she knows what she's doing with her career, and I hope she gets the chance to take Diego's position, which is the position she wanted and the promotion opportunity that may never come. I would suspect that her being here with her direct supervisor, assigned to the Abby Woo kidnapping, may be on-the-job training as a lead investigating agent. Diego was here to oversee, suggest, and nudge her in the proper direction when appropriate. But things were seldom as they appear and being promoted to senior agent seemed below Brennan's abilities. If she worked for me, I would ensure she was on the fast track to a leadership position above senior agent.

After graduating from Sam Huston State University with a degree in criminal justice, Brennan had her choice of career opportunities. Every agency with an acronym, every branch of the military, and every covert organization within the United States Government coveted her. Why? There were two reasons. The first was a 4.0 grade average, along with graduating number one in her class. The second was because she had something that could not be taught—her charm. It loosened up the people she spoke with and made them feel comfortable. It made them want to tell her everything in confidence, although it would never be kept secret. That adage, *she could sell ice to an Eskimo,* was truer of Brennan than anyone. And that's why I needed her; Brennan could get me what I needed easier than I could. No matter who she talked to at any level of authority, they just told her what she wanted to know without her directly asking for it. I needed her to get every possible piece of information on Taine that she could. Good, bad, indifferent—I needed it all.

I needed to know what Taine knew, so I asked her to double back on the FBI's information and the check every letter-name agency. I asked her if she could get Taine's history from her teenage years until now. I wanted to know what she knew about Abby and how she knew it. I needed to know why they had taken Abby from the bank, and I needed to prove the kidnapped Abby from the bank wasn't my Abby. If Brennan could find an acorn under all those leaves, I could prove my theory.

Brennan looked at me as if to sarcastically say, Is that all? Then she told me she had contacts in the Immigration and Naturalization Service, The Texas branch of the FBI, the Mexican Federales, and that she knew a guy who knew a guy in Homeland Security who she would hit up for a favor. She said she even had an old flame who now worked for NCIS, and although he was a navy cop, he would do anything she needed him to. I'm sure Brennan never had a problem getting a favor from any guy she asked. The only thing she wanted from me in return was the answer to one question; would she ever have a chance?

"If I didn't have Abby in my life and I had met you under different circumstances, maybe you'd have a chance."

A quick hint of disappointment flashed in her eyes then vanished as quickly as it came.

"We may have never met Brennan, and I hope you know why this can't happen."

Brennan took a deep, a calming breath, smiled and kissed me on the cheek. "Thanks' Paolo." Brennan went to leave without another word, and I thought I saw a tear in her eye.

"Hey, Brennan. Why is this so important to you? Tell me, so I understand what's going on with you."

Brennan turned around and came toward me as she wiped the corner of her eye with her pinky. "Every relationship I've had since high school ended badly—name calling, screaming at each other, physical fights, and once… once I almost killed a man. We were engaged, and, when I came home from a field assignment, I found him fucking my roommate. He had me so angry that I pulled my service weapon and put it to his head. I was so close to pulling the trigger . . . I'm not sure what stopped me. They ran out of the room and left me crying there like a baby." She had teared up from the pain of the memory. "That was my first year in the marshal service. If it wasn't a coworker, there would have been charges, but he told the review board that, as my supervisor, he had taken advantage of me. I got a reprimand in my file, and he was transferred out. I haven't seen him since, but it's still painful."

I felt the string of tears on her face and the pain in her words. "Jane, I never led you on."

"No, you didn't. That's why it's so damn important—being around you feels so natural, like I don't have to work at a relationship for once and that it would just happen on its own." She inhaled deeply. "I feel like this job is who I am, and that's why I never date anyone or have any relationships. It reminds me of what my dad always says. 'Jane, men don't like a woman who is headstrong, especially a woman in authority.' God, Paolo! Do you know what it's like to be alone every night?"

"I do. I was alone until I met Abby. I was alone for a few years after my discharge, then I met her. From the moment I saw her, I knew I loved her. Jane, I love her more than anything I can think of. She's all I think about. I thought I would never find anyone. I hope you find someone, like I have. You just need to let it happen."

Brennan stood with her palms on my chest. "Thanks for listening, Paolo. Abby is a lucky woman. I wish I were her. I wish I had you. I know I could love you." She leaned in like she would kiss me.

I gently grabbed both her hands and softly pushed her away. "This cannot happen. I won't let it. I love Abby, and I will not lose that, even for you. So please stop what you are doing."

Brennan pulled away and wiped her face with both hands.

"You're a beautiful woman—strong, determined, and smart. Any man would be lucky to have you. When this is over, put the job aside for a while. Go on vacation and enjoy yourself for once. Go back to Texas and see your parents. Talk to your mom about—better yet, talk with your father about your relationships with men, and, for God's sake, stop seeking his approval for every man you date."

Tears flowed again from Brennan's blue and reddened eyes. I had hit the sore spot, the reason for all her failed relationships—her father's disapproval of any man she brought home, no one was ever good enough for his baby girl. Her demeanor changed instantly as she went from being open and vulnerable to a level of anger, I'm willing to bet only one other man in the world had experienced, that man had a gun to his head.

She slapped my face with an open palm, and it hurt more than any man had ever hurt me. The level of pain was twofold—the physical pain was one thing, but the pain I have for making Brennan feel like that hurt too deeply to explain with words. Maybe it was the disappointment I saw in her eyes at what I had said about her father and hinting she would never find anyone good enough. I'm not sure, but I was hurting, and I was the cause of her pain.

When this is over, I'll sit Brennan's ass down and talk about the real reasons she had bitch-slapped me when I mentioned her father. Of course, I'll ask Abby for her approval and thoughts on the matter first. Maybe the three of us can discuss what happened, or maybe not. Somehow, I get the feeling Abby will think talking with Brennan about relationship issues is not a good idea.

Twelve

The Birth of Taine

Taine was not her given name; it could not be, because
Taine was a man's name. In its original form, Tian, meant
Man, God of the Forests. Throughout the years, the name
Tian was Americanized into *Taine.* It was not because of
how she said her name, it was more of how people heard
her pronounce it. A female born in China would never be
given a male name, let alone such a strong, masculine, and
enduring one. Lastly, as a woman, she would never be
placed in charge of or be allowed to oversee such an
important branch of the Triad.

At the time of her birth, women were not treasured
in China, and parents who had a female child often gave
them up for adoption, secretly hoping someone in another
country would love and care for their offspring. The male
heir was the important member of the family; he had to
carry on the family name and its honor. Families
considered females to be second-class citizens or
something worse, property for them to offer for sale.
Without a second thought, the father, the head of the
household, would often sell his daughter to a man of wealth
and means. Sometimes this was done for money or for the
rights to farm a piece of land or settle a debt. Taine, in a
previous life, was such a soul.

Agent Brennan had called in every favor, every
marker, and had to make promises of future favors to get
the information she did. Information on Taine was harder to

get than something classified top secret from the state department.

Without a date of birth for Taine, the best we could figure was she was more than seventy years old, if not older. Brennan had managed to get information about her from the most unlikely source. She had talked her way into Greaterford Prison with that sweet Texas accent and spoke with Taine's main adversary, someone she knew from the old country, someone she hated with every fiber of her being; the man who had changed her into who she is now—Chang Lo.

For the first time in her life, Brennan could not get her way with her Texas charm. Chang Lo was interested in spending time with the only person who had visited him in many years. She tried to steer the conversation in one direction, but Lo was better at Brennan's game than Brennan was. He had managed to stall her for two hours before he told his story of Taine's emergence as dragon head and replacing him as the leader of the east coast branch of the American Triad.

Chang Lo said he was lucky to be alive and that every day for the past fifty-five years he had contemplated why he was left alive to suffer the daily drudgery of time. Brennan said Lo looked as old as Taine, if not older than Taine, if that was possible. The normal succession of power within the Triad was the death of the dragon head whether by natural causes, such as old age, or, in the case of Lo, an assassination attempt that left him hospitalized and on the edge of death.

****

Taine was known to Lo as *Lien Bo*—or *precious lotus.* She had once been his property. He had purchased her through a slave trader, who had bargained with her father, in China as a fifteen-year-old kitchen maid. As with all female slaves within the house of Lo, He expected her to surrender herself to his sexual whims. Lien Bo fought off his advances every day, and, as a gentleman, Lo waited patiently for her to submit willingly, until he finally had enough of her resistance. The house held a late summer dinner party to celebrate Lo's promotion to incense master. His intoxication and his slaves' refusal to service one of his superiors overshadowed the celebration. How could they trust him to be a leader of men if he could not control a lowly female?

Lo was only two ranks below dragon head now, and he needed to prove he was capable of such a simple task. He said he begged forgiveness from the dragon head, who was in attendance for this dishonor, and vowed to correct the problem. Having consumed several bottles of wine, which gave him a severe headache, he had no tolerance for another refusal of favors from Lien Bo. Later that night, as she served him his nightly tea in his bed chamber, he insisted she disrobe and do what he demanded of all his female slaves. She refused for the last time.

Chang Lo became enraged and beat her into semi-consciousness. He tied her wrists to the bed and forced her into sexual submission until she was no longer present in her own body. Lo had an exaggerated feeling of power over

Lien Bo because of the beatings he gave her each time he forced himself on her.

Lien Bo awoke the next morning bruised and battered with only one thought in mind—live another day. She was not allowed to leave the bed chamber for almost three weeks, until Lo tired of the game and of Lien Bo. He had taken advantage of her inability to defend herself and abused her as many times a day as he could, if it wasn't him, it was one of his lieutenants who shamed her.

Some months later she was with child, and Lo allowed the baby to come to full term with the hope it would be male and could carry on his name as custom requires. The child was female, and Lo killed the baby moments after birth as Lien Bo watched in horror. Being left barren from complications fostered more hatred for her situation and for all the men who had forced this life upon her. Chang Lo said this event had changed Lien Bo into the cold killer she was today.

After her recovery from child-birth, Lo sent her to work in the stables on the outskirts of the property. Lo planned to never see her again. At this time, Lo was still a mid-level player in the triad, serving at the will of those in Hong Kong. But, with his ruthlessness, he was a fast riser in the organization's hierarchy. Prior to his relocation to America, Lien Bo had attempted to kill Lo. He said his guards were unaware of her escape from the stables and that she had hidden within a ditch along-side the path where he took his daily meditative walks. Once he had passed, she jumped out and stabbed him repeatedly in the back. He never saw his attacker, but he felt her revenge in each knife thrust. With her last bit of anger, Lien Bo stabbed Lo's right hand lying on a large, downed tree branch, impaling him to the branch as he screamed the way she had when he beat her into submission before he had forced himself on her.

Lo's guards heard his screams, and, as he passed out form the pain, the guard dragged Lien Bo to the stables and tied her up, so she could not escape again. Normally, Lo would have inflicted a slow, torturous death, but he said he felt sorry for her because of all the pain he had caused her. It was a rare moment of compassion from a ruthlessly uncompassionate man.

He ordered her tied naked to a post in the middle of the thatched stable. She could only walk in circles, with her left hand tied to the post, and even if she reached out her right hand, she could not touch the hut walls. Weakened by the lack of food from the once-a-day meager rations, she had no energy or the will to fight off any of Lo's subordinates. She was used as a sex slave and forced to do things no woman should have to do. Lien Bo was now nothing more than a way for Lo's men to release their anxiety from the stresses of following Lo's orders. They visited her several times a day, and he employed many men. This continued for nine months with no hope of an end or escape. Lien Bo was a shell of who she once was. She showed no emotion during Lo's men's visits and withdrew so deep into her own mind that she was no longer conscious of what they did to her.

Soon, Lo had assigned a new guard to the stable—a pawn in the organization—and his only job was to watch

Lien Bo. He became infatuated with her, seeing a woman naked for the first time, and soon forced himself onto her too. But he was different; he still had feelings of right and wrong and had not yet become the emotionless killer he needed to be to move up in the industry.

Things changed for Lien Bo. This new guard confessed his love for her—she had been his first encounter—and he lost all sense of loyalty to Lo. He gave her extra rations and water, and soon her strength returned with the aid of medications he snuck into her food. As time progressed, so did his love for her.

After he weaned her off the medications as directed by his supplier, Lien Bo could think with a clear head. She formulated a plan and put it into motion, only sacrificing the dignity she no longer had. She played along with him, letting him enjoy his almost daily ritual. She gained his confidence by pretending to enjoy his touch and the time he spent with her—both personally and sexually.

Each time he was with Lien Bo, he would remove his clothing and fold them neatly in a pile by the post she was tied to. The last thing he did was place his ceremonial knife on top of the clothes. It was his prize passion, the only thing he owned other than his clothing. Lim Fong, the leader of the district's triad, had gifted it to him on the day he accepted enlistment into the fold. His belief that Lien Bo loved him made him grow careless as she grew stronger, and that was the cause of his death at the hands of his lover.

On the night of celebration when Chang Lo was declared as the dragon head of the American branch of the

Triad, Lien Bo put her plan into its final stage. As he enjoyed what would be his last minutes of life, he did not see Lien Bo reach to the pile of clothing and take the knife. Just as he reached his peak, she stuck the knife into his throat, effectively silencing him while cutting the carotid artery. It took only minutes for him to die—excruciating minutes of suffocation and confusion. He died with his eyes wide open, fixed on the woman who he thought loved him. A look of complete shock and surprise remained on his face as a death mask.

Lien Bo took the bloodied knife and cut herself free of the ties. Her wrist was callused from the months of the rope burning her as she walked circles within her prison. She looked at the dead man, spat on him and cursed the house of Lo as she fled into the night, wearing only the shirt of the man she had just killed. She intended to get to the port and board any ship leaving Hong Kong harbor for any destination.

Lien Bo found refuge on a small farm outside of Hong Kong proper. She was still disoriented from her months of captivity, and, in the torrential rains, she became confused and lost her way. She was overcome and finally passed out from exhaustion. The next morning, a farm hand found her in the field and brought her to the main house and its owners. They cared for her during her healing and her final withdrawal from the drugs that had kept her alive. At times, they placed a gag in her mouth to keep her quiet, so no one outside would hear her screams and possibly tell the authorities about a worthless woman found on a property she had no business being on.

She stayed at the farm for twelve months—the last six she worked in the fields to repay her debt to the property owner, which she owed him for his care and sustenance. The last day of the year, he took her to the Port of Hong Kong, and, upon entry onto the ship, they told the captain that she was the daughter of the nephew of the farm owner. Her being sent away was repayment for a debt her father owed, to be the wife of a man who her father had owed money. In reality, it didn't matter what story he told; no one ever investigated the background of a female.

Lien Bo bowed and thanked the farm owner for his hospitality. He called her close and hugged her like she was his own daughter. He held her hand as he gave her one piece of wisdom he had learned throughout the years— revenge was never a way to achieve peace with oneself. Again, she bowed and thanked him; she kept her head down as she turned from him and his advice.

The smile she gave him was the last she would ever smile and the last time she would ever be called *Lien Bo*. She vowed from that day forward, she would be known to the world as Taine, and, with that name, she would exact revenge on Chang Lo and remove anyone who stood in her way. This was the beginning of her rise to power, a rise that would lead her to reconnecting with her tormentor in a land neither of them knew.

For her first night on the ship, the captain assigned her to work in the kitchen. He instructed the cook to use her as he saw fit. She was once again a slave to a man, but this time it was a necessary evil. The other galley workers regarded her as an intrusion into their close-knit group.

They teased her unmercifully, and, when they asked her name, she told them directly, "My name is Taine." They mocked her and called her names, like *whore* or a word in Chinese the meant *unwanted pig.* They also contemplated taking advantage of a young woman with no male escort, but those thoughts vanished quickly as the captain had discovered information about a murdered assistant cook on her second night abord the ship bound for America. Another cook had witnessed Taine murder his mate, and once the crew knew the truth, no one bothered her again.

As before, she had killed using the knife she had plunged into the throat of a man—the same short thrust into his neck as he lay on top of her. It was simple and effective; let him think he was getting his way and then the death blow would come. The second cook had later confessed to the captain that he had thrown the body overboard to hide what had happened and to avoid any more problems in the galley. He also told his boss that Taine looked directly at him as she licked the blood from the knife, as a way of striking fear into the cook's heart.

The next morning, as she entered the galley, she looked into the eyes of the man who saw her murder his mate. He lowered his gaze and went about his duties. The rest of the crew parted as she headed toward her workstation. They would not report her, or the true story of the murder, to the captain, because the men were too frightened to speak against her. She remained alone for the rest of the voyage, and no one else disappeared from the ship.

Chang Lo took a deep breath and stopped the story. Brennan asked if she should know anything else about Taine. He told her that he had been in one prison or another for almost sixty years, and she was his first visitor. Then he asked if she would remain in the presence of an old man, so he could gaze upon such a beautiful young woman. She allowed him to trace her body with his eyes, a favor for finishing his story. It took great restraint for her not to say anything, as she felt what Taine must have felt so long ago. Continuing his story, he said Taine had arrived in America as she had left China—completely unknown and alone. She had snuck off the ship under the cover of a moonless night, and no one ever acknowledged that she had ever been on the ship.

Brennan asked Lo if the reason he had been sent to America was because of Lien Bo. He told her Lien Bo had embarrassed him in front of his boss on more than one occasion. He added that normally they would have prohibited his rise in the organization, but his direct boss—now an assistant dragon head—was who had recruited him. To keep the embarrassment to a minimum, they had promoted him to dragon head and forced him to relocate to America. It was an out of sight, out of mind action for his boss and those above him.

Taine's rise to power was unique because she was female and because of her young age. She took advantage of every opportunity. She was cruel to those that did not align themselves with her—she would make them one offer for them to join her group, and if they declined, they were dead by noon the next day. Many of the triads' minor members and a few of the more important members disappeared. The triad leaders were stunned to learn that Taine was a woman, and its ripples were felt throughout the organization and all the way to Hong Kong.

The one thing the leaders of the triad feared most was her ruthless disregard for the governing rules of their male-dominated organization. She would kill anyone at any level, no matter who they were or what their status was. After several attempts on her life failed and many important men in the organization went missing, the leadership in Hong Kong gave orders to make peace with Taine. They dispatched Won Koi, the next man in line to lead the entire triad, to America to do so.

The two met very briefly—less than five minutes—at the Ritz Carlton in Philadelphia. They sipped tea and immediately got down to business. When Koi asked Taine what she wanted, she told him that she wanted to remove Lo from power and to be dragon head for the east coast . . . for now. Koi agreed, he stood and bowed then left the way he entered, facing Taine.

Chang told Brennan the real reason he was still alive was because the police were only two blocks away when the assignation attempt took place. Patrolmen heard the gunfire and arrived quickly with the ambulances arriving moments later. Lo was in surgery within minutes of the shooting. He was hit twelve times, and because of what he says is karma, not one bullet hit a vital organ.

After his recovered, a grand jury tried him for racketeering and murder. The Superior Court judge ordered him to multiple life sentences. A moment after the sentencing he learned of Taine's identity and of her presence in the United States. The look on his face, one of recognition, came too late as the bailiff approached to escort him to the holding cell. He spoke her name in a whisper as he passed. "Lien Bo!"

Taine sat in the front row of the court room with no fear of repercussions. She owned the judge and the court. She regarded Lo with smug satisfaction and a cold glare. A briefcase remained on the bench next to Taine. The district attorney grabbed it on his way out of the court room. It was payment for Lo's conviction—a cool million for the DA as well as the judge.

"That's an interesting tale," Brennan told Lo. "But how do you know all the details so factually? I mean, it's not like you followed Taine around all the time."

Lo smiled at Brennan's naïve question. "I thought better of you, Marshal Brennan. Surely you must know Taine visited me after my conviction and enlightened me on every detail of her life, since the day she tried to kill me."

"But with all your connections, you couldn't get a reduced sentence or at least be moved to general population, for the company of others."

"I remain here for one reason, Marshal, to stay alive. As long as I am in solitary confinement, Taine will let me live. She will allow me to think of all I had done to her as a young girl, to remember each of the beatings I gave her and the pleasures I took from her. It is my penance, like the man from your Bible story, where he pushed the boulder to the top of the mountain and, just as he got it there, your God would make it roll to the bottom again. This is my hell, Marshall Brennan.”

Brennan said her cell rang at that instant. She pulled it out of her jacket pocket and viewed the name and number on the screen. Her face reddened with anger.

“Bad news, Marshal?”

She didn’t answer and tried to turn the tables. “In other words, you’re hiding from Taine. A man like you, with your background, fears a worthless woman?”

“Yes! I’m hiding from Taine and more importantly, from Lien Bo. One was the purest form of innocence and the other, Taine, is the purest form of evil—an evil I created, and that scares even me, Marshal Brennan.”

Thirteen

On the Run

At this point, I still had no idea how Abby was tied into all this. I thought she was just a young woman who loved music so deeply that she changed her course in life to live her dream. Now what I need to do is find her and find the reason why our lives have been turned upside down into this improbable mess. It's time for me to do what I've always done best—complete the mission at hand. I haven't done so in quite some time other than earning a buck here and there. But it's like riding a bike; you get on, fall off a few times and then you're on your way down the block like you never even stopped riding.

Abby meant the world to me, and I wasn't about to lose that. And the gang who did this to her . . . well, frankly the way I feel right now, they'll pay with their lives, and yes, Mr. Philbin, that *is* my final answer. I've killed before in the service of my country, and I will do it again, need be, to save the one thing I love the most. Abby was the only person I have ever told about what I had done in the military, and, after hearing some of the details, she made me promise that no matter what I would never kill again. It was a condition of our engagement; she said she could not live with a man who had such disregard for human life.

Abby really was naïve about the ways of the world, but I'm sure she has changed her mind. I know killing is wrong, but, as I've said before, "When I have to answer for what I have done, I will stand before the Creator and accept whatever punishment he bestows on me." Like beauty, evil is in the eye of the beholder. We tell ourselves the evil we are doing is necessary for the good of all humanity. It may be a way for us to feel good about what we do, but the truth is, you can't fight evil with tolerance and understanding.

I told Brennan that we wouldn't be returning to the warehouse, but I had a small change in mind, I wanted to gear up for an urban operation. Fighting in the desert or jungle was different than pulling off an op in the city or in a populated setting, and this was a somewhat domestic episode. If the police caught me doing what I was about to do, I couldn't help Abby, and a domestic terrorism charge would be a death blow; it would mean life in prison with no chance of parole. Domestic terrorism falls under the Patriot Act; there wouldn't even be an official trial, just a conviction. I would be buried so deep in the federal system that I would never see daylight again.

I know this level of thinking, or this level of planned violence as an operation for a kidnap victim rescue seems a bit ridiculous, but Taine is triad and extremely ruthless, plus she had the advantage of having her fingers in every pie the city was baking. The triad, also known as the White Lotus Society, is far worse than the Mexican cartel, and the Mexicans were some bad motherfuckers. White Lotus had an estimated one and a half million members in mainland China alone. They were into every type of crime imaginable—weapons, drugs, money laundering, and, of course, the sex trade. This group was responsible for trafficking young girls around the world. They offered wealthy men a smorgasbord of females and would sell the girls for a huge profit. Men, like the Mullah of Iran, a supposed Holy Man, would pay a king's ransom for stealing the virtues of a young virgin, no matter her race. If Abby was destined to be someone's property, it would devastate me.

The triad was notorious for their lack of feelings for anyone outside their organization. Members were required, upon initiation, to follow and strictly adhere to the thirty-six oaths. In a ritualistic ceremony, they swore their oath in the blood of a sacrificed animal. After walking beneath raised swords while reciting the thirty-six oaths, the paper that holds the written words is burnt on the altar, confirming the new members obligation to the triad. Taine never swore the blood oath, she never intended to follow any bylaws or any orders from her so-called superiors, and she would never be sworn to the servitude that she had suffered as a young girl. She had her own set of laws or oaths, which she never deviated from, no matter what. The one oath Taine live by was "Do unto others." She didn't ask her men to martyr themselves, like the Soldiers of Islam; her soldiers would just kill you and then go home, as if they were punching the clock at some factory job.

Brennan had acquired a lot of information about Taine, more than we really needed. Chang Lo's only interest was keeping Brennan with him for as long as he possible could. Technically, Taine was a deputy dragon head, but she ruled as if she was the mountain master—the number one man, so-to-speak. With that being true, Abby was in some major shit. Since Taine had her fingers in every organization, she held several federal authorities in her grasp, and things like a request for help with a missing person would be lost in the system. I'm sure by now Taine knows who I am, if she hadn't already.

I opened the Sea Box container and pushed my motorcycle past the car I had borrowed from the safe house. I packed up what I thought I would need into a go-bag and strapped it to the rear of the Ninja. Abby said this bike was my kryptonite and I needed to get rid of it. That's why I hid the Kawasaki Ninja Super Sport—ZX-14R—at the warehouse, just in case I wanted to take an adrenaline-infusing ride. It was green, and it was mean, it was fast, and it was furious. Nothing more than a politically incorrect rice-burner for speed when you needed it in a tight spot.

I pushed the bike outside the warehouse, returned to the building and entered a code, Abby's birthday, on the keypad. The doors closed and the panel beeped with eight indicator lights, signifying the two charges on the SEA BOX's and the six on the warehouse support columns were active. My plan was to remove any evidence of what was in the containers and revenge on a car maker that would produce such a piece of crap like a MiEV.

I mounted the bike as I put on the sleek green helmet, brought the engine to life and drove toward the exit gate. As I left the complex, a soft hiss came from behind me and then the loud sound of a building collapsing on itself. I rode for almost one mile before emergency vehicles passed me going the direction I had come from.

Twenty minutes later, I wheeled the bike to the curb along Delaware Avenue. I took out a burner cell and dialed Brennan's number. She answered on the first ring.

I briefed her with what Richards had told me was in the file he had on Abby. She didn't like it; it sounded overly complicated and a bit farfetched. I told her I didn't understand how Abby could have been returning from China while she was doing time at CHOP as a resident, unless she had taken a bunch of time off to track down her family. The more I thought about it, the more it didn't make sense.

Standing on the side of the road, I recalled the day in the bank vault. She was looking at the parchment that held the family tree, as if it was the first time she'd seen it. When she put on the necklace, it was as if she were trying on a very expensive piece of jewelry at some store; she held it in her palm and gazed at its beauty. Then she separated the gold chain with each hand and slipped the necklace over her head. As always, I held up her hair as she adjusted the necklace, so it sat just in the right spot on her chest. She kept her right hand on it as she smiled at the satisfaction of feeling its weight against her skin. A loud horn brought me back to reality, and I heard Brennan calling my name.

"DeLuca? You still there? Hello?"

"Yeah, sorry."

"Where are you?"

"Still in the city."

"What's the plan? Where you headed?"

"It's better you don't know." I knew she'd find a way to come along.

"I want to help you find Abby. You know that, right?"

"Yeah, that's why I'm not telling you."

"Hey, DeLuca. Come on. You know I have some damn good skills."

"I'll find a place to holed up for the night and then move out early tomorrow morning."

"You're going to see Taine at the grocery store to find out what she did with Abby. I can meet you there."

"It's better if you don't Brennan."

The phone was silent for a long time before she agreed, but I knew she would come anyway.

"Tell you what, Brennan, I'll call when I need your help." I knew that was bullshit and so did she.

She was pleading her case as I disconnected the line. I couldn't watch Brennan's six—protect her—while I was looking for Abby. If something happened to Brennan, like the fact that I knew Taine would kill her just because she could, I would have to live with that pain for the rest of my life, and I already had enough pain for two lifetimes.

Getting back on the bike, I headed for the seedier side of an already bad part of the city. I paid cash for a room in a flophouse that looked like somewhere Norman Bates would feel right at home.

I gave the owner an extra fifty and told him, "I'm not here."

He said, "No one ever is."

In this part of town, a guy could get himself killed for just looking at someone else the wrong way. The only thing that mattered in this area was the color of your money. It spoke to people, with a voice that said, "Here, now shut the hell up and leave me the fuck alone." The old phrase *money talks and bullshit walks* probably originated in a place just like this and for reasons just like this.

I pushed the bike toward room number six where I found a homeless man pacing between rooms one and ten, as if he were pulling guard duty on the hotel. He looked at me, and I nodded in greeting. I spoke to him with the respect I would expect from another man. "Excuse me sir, I'm in need of some services, which I think you can provide. Are you interested?"

He approached me and introduced himself as Montgomery James Pittamore. As he shook my hand he said, "Friends call me *Pitt.* What's you got for me that I can helps you with?"

"I need you to stand watch for the night. If you see anything you think is abnormal, knock on the door once and say, 'Ely's coming.'"

"Ely's commin. Hide jore heart, girl! Simple nuff, but I need to see the cash up front. Cash money or it's no dice, my friend."

I pulled a wad of cash from my pocket and handed him two one hundred-dollar bills.

"Not's to be greedy, but there is a service charge for my undivided attention."

I slipped him another hundred and his smile showed no teeth but all joy. After tonight, he would have enough money to keep him in cheap liquor for a month.

"Are we good?"

He turned and walked to a grocery cart stacked high with a collection of anything he had ever found on the streets. He returned with a gray plastic milk crate, turned it upside down and sat it between doors five and six. His actions answered my question. He perched on the milkcrate as if he were sitting on a royal throne and gazing upon his court.

"Don't worry none. This here street king gots your back, Mr. Money Bags. If you needs anything else, I's only a hundred dollars away."

I unlocked the door to the room, entered and rearranged the furniture—some of this shit Goodwill wouldn't even except for a donation. I went back outside, started up the bike, and backed it into the motel room.

"What in the hell you doin' with your motorbike in da house?"

"Come on, Pitt. Don't you recognize love? I can't sleep without her." I closed the door and gave a twist to the almost—dead deadbolt.

I moved the one overstuffed chair to the back wall opposite the door. I sat with my feet propped on the small end table and placed the M16 across my lap, locked and loaded and ready for any interruption. I had slept like this before, many nights leaning against the back of a teammate or a tree trying my best to blend into the background so my spotter and I could stay alive. As a member of any special forces group, one learned to stay awake and alert even as they teetered on the edge of drifting into the first stages of sleep.

I have learned how to adapt that level of alertness into a stage of conscious awareness even in the light stages of sleep. Sitting upright, feet extended and weapon in hand, I was now ready for what tomorrow may bring. With Pitt outside, I felt confident I would be safe until the first sunrays graced the morning sky, and I could relax knowing I have what Taine wants—a little black and red thumb drive containing all of her bought and paid for contacts. She'd kill to get it back but not until she knew exactly who had it and their plans for it. That meant Abby would stay alive until Taine has the drive in her possession. It afforded me the opportunity to get a few hours rest and to start the day on my terms—reaching my destination around sunrise and an opportunity to survey the general area.

Awakening as the first dull streams of sunlight peeked through the yellow cigarette-smoke-stained curtain, I saw the quietness that was the early morning of the city outskirts. Standing, stretching, yawning, and breathing to fully awaken myself, I readied for the day. I removed everything from the go-bag and strategically placed them on the bike. I tucked the M16 within the sleeve on the right side just below the seat and the M40 Sniper Rifle on the left side. My auto-pistol had a twelve round clip locked inside and a chambered round for a slight advantage if needed. The Ninja was all geared up and ready for me to mount it and power it into action.

Feeling rejuvenated, I recalled the night's events. In my meditation to prepare for rest, I had felt Abby's presence, telling me she was alive and where she was. Her message was simple: "You know where to find me, Paolo." Closing my eyes, I clearly saw the place where they had taken her—a place we had been before. Knowing that now, as a fact, all anxiety dissipated, as it had when I was in Abby's arms.

Opening the door to the day ahead, the world revealed a cool, damp morning. The sun was still low, peeking its head above the Earth, as if it were trying to sneak up on the world. The mist surrounding the city was repelling its warmth, which was almost a living example of the anxiety I felt earlier. The Street King was still perched upon his throne keeping vigil over me, like the Guardian Angel Michael, the archangel of miracles and protection. Today, I would need both from Michael—protection to do what I needed and a miracle to safely return Abby home.

As I pushed the Ninja outside, the burner cell rang—only two people had the number, and, after last night's conversation, it could not be Brennan calling.

"Yeah?" I answered without regard for formality.

"I got a copy of the surveillance video from the bank vault. It's all footage of the day of the robbery. This is some high-end shit for a city bank, DeLuca. It has audio as well as video.

"And . . . ?"

He asked more specifically about Abby and me being in the vault, why were we there. I told him the same story I told everyone who asked me about that day, at least what I remembered.

"What did Abby do just before the explosion?"

I thought it was an odd question. I had just explained what we were there for. I asked a question in answer to a question. "What do you mean, what did she do."

Richards hesitated, probably trying to formulate a response so it didn't sound accusatory. "It's not good, brother. Abby covered her head, turned and leaned away from you just seconds before the blast occurred, like she knew it was coming. Do you remember that happening, DeLuca?"

I had replayed that event in time so many times that each second of the memory film footage was an imprinted snapshot, but some of those snapshots were out of focus and unidentifiable. "Not fully."

"Here's the scenario. The video shows you two at a desk of some kind. Miss Woo takes the necklace from the deposit box, after which she closes the box and slips the mag-key into her pocket."

"Still not telling me anything, Richards. Times getting short, and I've got to move."

"The woman in the video . . . I have a gut feeling about her."

"You're telling me you think she was in on it?"

"I'm saying it's like there was some kind of signal before she moved away from you. She moves, and if you count down—like two . . . one—*boom,* the explosion happens."

I told him every line I could think of to disprove his theory—how she acted, what she said, how she moved. *Moved . . .* "The back of her shirt lifted as she moved around just before the explosion. I don't remember seeing the tattoo on her back." It was more of a question-slash-what-the-hell-am-I-seeing type statement.

"It gets worse, I keep replaying sections of the surveillance video. I had it enhanced because the microphones in the vault sustained some damage. She said to the guy pulling the chain from around her neck, 'You're not taking the necklace.' Now, in my professional opinion, I think someone that protective of a piece of expensive as shit piece of jewelry would have said, 'You're not taking *my* necklace.' See where I'm going here, DeLuca?"

"I do, but I don't like it."

"Like I said before, smells like shit. Call it a gut feeling but I don't think it was a slip of the tongue. Sorry to break the news to you, DeLuca, but this Abby, the one in the video, was part of the gang."

"That just proves that the girl in the bank, the one in the video, is not my Abby."

"You still think they are two different women and the one in the vault was taking your girlfriends place for some reason?"

"Not for some reason, for *a* reason."

"I'm starting to agree with you, DeLuca. The more I go over this thing, the less sense it makes, and that makes any scenario possible."

"I have a theory."

"Want to enlighten me?"

"Can't prove shit yet."

"Okay, DeLuca. I'll go with your gut on this. I know mine has served me well in the past. Last thing, before I let you go. I got your back, no matter how this goes down."

I disconnected the call before either of us could say another word.

Fourteen

Pennville

I should have realized sooner where to look for Abby; she had a tie to the place I didn't understand one bit. Pennville State School and Hospital held a fascination for her, and it was kind of our real first date and the place where we first . . . you know. Abby and me she had snuck onto the property on several occasions and explored the dilapidated and antiquated buildings that housed the patients. Well, *housed* was a polite term for *locked up and drugged into submission.*

Now Abby was a lot of things but being politically correct was not one of them. She just said whatever was on her mind without regard for how it sounded. Don't get me wrong, she didn't say things to be hurtful; she said them because they were true, and, in most cases, they were. During our first visit to Pennville together, we went into one of the doctor's offices, and she pulled this broken wooden chair next to a nasty brown sofa with missing cushions. After placing down a blanket, she had me lay on the sofa, and she sat back in the wooden chair, crossing her legs, and pretended to smoke a pipe or cigar.

Abby did the worst impression of Sigmund Freud I have ever heard. She said, "Mr. Smitt, after carefully studying your case, I have come to the undeniable conclusion that you are fucking crazy!"

I busted out laughing, which sent her into hysterics, and that's what led to our first romantic kiss, I kept laughing as she repeatedly poked me in the head with her forefinger while speaking in that bad accent and leaning close to me. When her face was just inches from mine, things stopped for an eternity, and that's when I kissed her. She recoiled for a moment, as if pondering life on earth, and then leaned in and kissed me.

I pulled her toward me, and she moved willingly, lying on top of me in the moment of full emotion. We didn't speak another word for the next hour or so, but all the talking was done with deliberate touch and passionate love. It was the best experience with a woman I have ever had, and that was because I was so in love with her.

She laid on top of me, emotionally spent, eyes closed, and softly breathing. I could feel the rise and fall of her chest with each passing breath. Suddenly, with a soft voice as she exhaled, she said, "Wow!"

Lost in the magical memory, I stood in the rays of the warm, rising sun—hence the name of the boulevard the flophouse was on—and I must have stood there a bit too long for Street King's liking.

He spoke to me with such interest, "What choo think' 'bout?"

"A woman."

"She mus be an aaful spessil women to make you smile like dat when she ain't even here!" He snickered while slapping the top of his leg to emphasize the joy he felt at seeing how much I cared for another person. "I tell you dis brodda. You grab hold to dat woman an' tell her to her heart how much love you gots inside for her. My wife use to sez to me 'fore she pass, 'Baby. I loves ya to da moon and back,' and dat ain't somein' you just find anywhere now." He hung his head and cried a few tears and spoke quietly to his deceased wife. "I miss you baby."

"Well, Pitt . . ." I was at a loss for words because of the grief I felt emanating from his soul. "She is special, more than anything else in the world."

I felt like I was saying confession to a priest—but one who was sitting upon a gray milkcrate. When I knelt in front of Pitt and asked him why he was out here, he raised his eyes, and I looked deep into his soul and found a unique peace within it.

He said one more thing to me in a rare moment of clarity, as if he were a different person, "I'm not living out here because I'm homeless. I'm living out here because, without my sweets, there's no reason to go home."

How could a man with nothing have everything? I smiled, stood, and reached to shake his hand.

He stood heavily from the crate, and, with a grasp powerful enough to crush whatever it held, he wrapped his hand around mine and pulled me into his chest. He embraced me with his other arm as if I were his brother.

I returned the gesture. When he let go, I said, "Pitt, take this and buy you wife some flowers."

He took the hundred from my hand, nodded in understanding and turned from me thanking me for the memory of his wife. I had faith that Pitt would never speak of me being here.

I started the Ninja and the roar of pure speed drifted from the twin tail pipes, shattering the morning silence.

Pitt yelled in his street dialect as I left a trail of burnt rubber on the pavement, "*Woooo!* Dat's Nice!"

It was time to find Abby and put an end to this mystery for good.

*****

I put a lot of distance between me and the Rising Sun Motel as fast as I could. Turning off Rising Sun Boulevard and onto Delaware Avenue, I throttled up the Ninja to seventy-five in the forty-mile-per-hour zone. Two traffic lights ahead, I saw a Philly patrol car sitting catty corner to the street in the lot of some dilapidated building. Letting off the gas, the Ninja rolled to a stop just as the light turned red. I glanced in his direction through the helmets narrow, smoke-black lens. Not moving an inch, I saw from the corner of my eye that the light had turned green.

Giving the cycle gas, it rolled forward, and the cruiser's lightbar came to life . . . but only for an instant. They were off as suddenly as they were on, with no movement of the vehicle to follow. Maybe Richards put out the word; maybe he asked the traffic division not to chase some loon on a bike. Maybe, but I don't recall telling him about the ninja. Maybe he just knew in his gut this was exactly what I would be doing, because it was what he would have done. Again, maybe.

I arrived at the New Lin Chong Grocery minutes later. A large white box truck was parked out front, with the rear door rolled up and two bulky Asian guys pretending to unload it. *Pretending* . . . Who unloads a truck full of groceries in shiny black leather shoes and suit jackets? They didn't belong unloading trucks; they were gang muscle, pretending to fit in with the scene their boss had set.

I dismounted the bike after surveying the situation, figuring the threat existed whether I stayed here or went inside to see Taine. Approaching the store, I carried the helmet by its closed strap in my right hand as a just-in-case weapon. I had a pistol in my right boot, just within reach if I was knocked to the floor, and I had a backup weapon sewn into the Ninja jacket's right sleeve—an auto-expand baton. It was light, sleek, and made of titanium. Most importantly, the baton stung like a Portuguese man-o-war hiding under the ocean waves.

As I passed the open truck, the muscle head standing on the liftgate nodded in the direction of the door. I barely acknowledged his presence, trying to match his masculine bravado.

I entered, and another gentleman just as muscular greeted me. He frisked me and took the Glock I had stuffed in my jean's waist band; it was my bait weapon. He may have continued to frisk me if his partner hadn't walked in and spoke to him. He responded as if his partner had told him, *hurry up, she is waiting.*

When I stepped away, he grabbed my helmet. The strap kept the helmet in my possession as the buckle dug into my gloved hand.

With a slight accent, he said, "This stays here until you leave." I'm sure he knew what I would use it for if I needed to. If my grip on the helmet hadn't distracted him, he may have inspected the bulge in the wrist of the riding gear. Feeling satisfied I was no longer a threat, he told me to follow him to the rear of the store. Passing through a doorway that a bamboo curtain partially hid, we entered a storage area and found three people waiting for me.

The woman sat at the table while two young Asian gentlemen flanked her. Standing with their hands clasped at the waist, they looked like lethal twins all wound up and ready to pounce. Taine eyed the man to her left, and the two of them left the room without a word, but I'm sure they didn't go far. Taine appeared as if she had lived two lifetimes; she looked older than she was.

She spoke with a strength and clarity unexpected of someone her age. "Please sit and have some tea."

I accepted so as to not insult her cultural background. She poured each of us some tea, raised her cup in a toast, "To your health." I did the same.

"With the formalities over, let's get down to business. First let me say, the picture on your identification was very complimentary, Mr. DeLuca."

I must have shown a fleeting look of surprise, because a slight smile teased at the corners of her mouth.

"Yes, I know who you are. Did you think me so foolish? I knew your identification was fake the moment my men brought it to me. So, tell me, Mr. DeLuca, what do you need from me? Perhaps a better fake identification?"

"I need Abby."

"No."

I stood quickly without realizing the intent behind my action. Before I could rebut, the goons were on me instantly. I flicked my right arm down, and the baton extended to its full length. With no pause, I spun to the left, and, as the goon past me, I caught him in the back of the head with one blow, killing him instantly. As the second goon tried a jump kick, I side stepped and hit his extended knee with a hard, downward motion. We both heard it crack. He landed on the tiled floor, elbow first. I'm sure it broke, because he screamed in agony.

The man who had escorted me in came through the curtained door and grabbed me in a bear hug. He would break my ribs if I didn't get free soon. I threw my head backward into his face, and his blood spattered my neck. I brought my fist downward, striking his groin, just like I had been taught in special forces. He released me, and I stepped forward with my right foot as I brought my left foot behind me. The baton struck the man on the side of the face, and he knelt as I struck him with the full force of my rotation. When he toppled to the floor, I stomped on his head to ensure he would not get up again. He didn't.

The old woman had never moved from her seat at the table. Then she stood and spoke as if she had all the cards in her hand, even with her guards on the floor now useless. "I know who your Abby is, and I know what your Abby is, and your Abby is dead if I see you again. Do not go near Pennville, Mr. DeLuca, or Miss Woo will suffer an unkind death." Taine turned and left through the rear exit.

I reached the exit just as the door to a pearl-colored escalade closed. It sped off with an identical vehicle following it. As I watched them turn the corner at the end of the alley, at least I knew Abby was still alive.

Heading back out the front, I grabbed my helmet and the Glock from the counter. With my weapons back in place and my helmet on, I brought the bike to life and pushed the throttle to its limit.

When we meet again, I am sure they will be more aggressive toward me. If it's a fight they want, they got one. In less than an hour, I'll be in Spring City—home of Pennville State School—and it will be my turn to haunt the abandoned facility.

*****

New Lin Chong Grocery shrank to a speck in my rearview mirror. I laid the bike to the right, taking the ramp to Route 76 with the intention of breaking a land speed record and then got on Route 422. The Schuykill Expressway was never a good way to get around Philadelphia, and this morning, even at this early hour, it was tied up tight.

Some jackass in a Honda had wedged himself underneath a souped-up Dodge Ram pickup, and, if he had been going a bit faster, the trailer hitch would have been in his right ear. The road was squeezed to one lane, and the cars could barely pass on the right as the rubberneckers got an eye full of the accident. I moved the bike as far to the right as I could and navigated the almost non-existent shoulder. I passed an entire crowd of irate motorists and one fat Philly cop.

As I barely balanced the bike at such a low speed, the cop yelled and threw both hands over his head. I heard the all-telling South Philly accent as he called me a few names, most of them starting with the letter *F*.

Once I had snaked through the traffic, the lanes cleared, and I opened the throttle full. The bikes' top speed was one-hundred eighteen miles per hour. With a prayer, I got it up to one-twenty-five. I passed other vehicles like they were standing still, but it was more like they were never moving. Abby always said it was like I had a death wish when I rode the Ninja. She was right, its power and speed were just as addicting as the best narcotic. Once the first adrenaline rush dropped, you needed to feel it again, but you had to push the limits of the machine to get there.

I took the ramp to 422 at an angle so steep that the riding gear's knee pad dragged the pavement. I felt the road reaching up to grab me as it had once before, but this time I would not let it. The same type of outfit had saved my ass from some major road rash once before; the bike had fallen from under me as I had tried to avoid a semi making a left turn across traffic lanes in front of me. As the bike had jettisoned from under me, I slid just behind it, as if I were its shadow. The bike hit a pothole and went airborne. It flipped twice before it went halfway through the thin metal side of the trailer. Its rear wheel had hung out like a three-dimensional sign intended to stop someone from drinking and driving. I had escaped with a broken arm and a headache, but the bike had been trashed. A passerby had helped me to my feet and gawked at the bike and trailer. He kept repeating how lucky I was to be alive—if only he had known.

Slowing the Ninja to a modest twenty-five, I turned onto Service Road; the Pennville facility was just a few hundred yards ahead. I didn't see any movement, but that didn't mean no one was there.

I removed the burner cell from the zippered chest pocket and called Richards to ask if he could three-way Brennan on our conversation. He put me on hold to dial Brennan's cell. He came back on and said Brennan was also on the line.

"Good," I said. "I'll be making some noise very soon. If you want to join the party, come on over to Pennville, but I'm not waiting for anyone, so you may miss out on the fun."

"We're on our way," Brennan said. "Don't move until we get there, DeLuca."

I heard Richards yelling in the background to his boss, Chief, we'll need a SWAT team and EMS teams at Pennville!" As I disconnected the call, I heard Brennan say, "Shit!"

To the left of the entry gate was a sign advertising the haunted horrors now available for your experience during tours of the storied facility. Taine had purchased the property and turned it into a tourist trap. The sign hinted at state-of-the-art animatronics and the best sound system in the region' Disney would be jealous. I pulled the M40 sniper rifle from its resting place on the bike and looked through the eye piece, scoping the property for possible targets or threats. I found several.

A sentry was posted in the main building's attic. He was visible through the scope as he leaned against the wall, smoking a cigarette. His weapon was propped up against the opposite wall, an arm's reach away. Careless, I thought. A second man stood at the main entrance's double doors to the same building. He held his weapon by its hand grip as he cradled it across his chest, effectively blocking the center mass target and his heart. The third man stood watch at the main gate. He sat in a chair tilted back against the booth's wall, and his weapon lay across his lap. He was dozing and seemed not to care about his job. I'm guessing that was because they didn't see much activity here until the October holiday season begun. All of them had Uzis as weapons; they were effective, unless I took out the guards before I reached the entry gate, and that was the plan.

The guy in the attic was the first to fall. I put a round in his forehead, and he slid down the wall he was leaning against. The man at the front doors went the same way; his head snapped back as the round penetrated, and his body followed. The guy in the booth was still sleeping and didn't know he had died from a round through his heart. Three quiet *poofs* from the M40 eliminated three possible threats to my life; it was now somewhat safer to move in.

I tossed the helmet onto the ground as I slid the rifle into its sleeve on the side of the bike. I pulled the Glock and placed it inside of the open zipper of my jacket for easy access. I retrieved the M16 from the sleeve on the other side of the bike and then locked and loaded a banana clip into the receiver group of the weapon. The last thing I did was hide the flash drive within the Ninja's taillight. If caught, the guards would search me and everything I carried, looking for anything I may have on me. They would not search anything further on the bike once they had taken the weapons from it. I started the bike and headed to the entry gate, which I hoped was latched and not locked.

Stopping just outside the gate, I leaned forward and unlatched it. I pushed it hard, and it swung open, offering enough room for me to drive through with little effort. The sounds of the engine summoned two more guards from their hiding places. They fired as they ran toward me with no regard for their lives. I pulled the Glock from its resting place and returned fire, emptying the clip while moving the weapon left to right again. Both went down as I dropped the bike behind the pearl-colored Escalade. I put a round in two of its four tires.

Using it as cover, I peered over the hood. I saw no movement on the grounds, but that didn't mean no one else was there. Sprinting with a slight limp, I headed toward the front door. They still held the advantage with all the surveillance cameras, but that fact really didn't figure into the equation anyway. My mission was to get Abby and get out—or the least of my worries, get dead. This was an all or nothing scenario, and I had accepted the variables of either outcome. Without Abby, I had no reason to go on; that's how important she was to my life. Taine would surely kill us both if I failed, so I had nothing to be afraid of.

Leaning against the wall next to the front door, I peered around the corner, trying to see inside. Nothing was visible, and that meant they were now waiting for me to enter. I slowly pushed the door with my left hand, and automatic gunfire erupted. Several men firing Uzis at the door splintered it into something resembling a wooden and glass sieve.

I crouched low and fired two rounds, killing one gunman. Standing and kicking the door, it fell apart, allowing me access to the main hallway. A shadow ducked into one of the side offices as I stood still with minimal cover as my eyes adjusted to the light.

A door creaked as the gunman pried it open just enough to clear the barrel of the gun. Several shots danced around my feet as the old linoleum tile shattered and jettisoned into the air.

I crouched, aimed at the door, and squeezed off two more rounds in retaliation. I got up to move, and a round hit the center of where I had just been squatting. I thanked God for a small miracle.

As I moved toward the door, the gunman stepped through. I raised my weapon as he did. Two shots rang out simultaneously. His short tore my riding jacket, and my shot hit his thigh, dropping him to the ground. I approached him as he raised his weapon to fire. I had no choice but to kill a wounded man, in this instance, it was the only thing to do.

Building recon was my next move, and I had two choices. One was to stay on the main floor, and the other was to head to the next. I took option two. After a close inspection of several rooms, I located a door to the attic area. Once there, I found the guard who was now covered in blood from the round I had put in his head. The room contained some audio and video components, which I disabled to lessen their advantage. With the upper floors covered and cleared, I returned to the ground floor and checked any room I came across. I found nothing or no one waiting for me. Odd. The door at the end of the hallway offered frosted glass with black lettering that read, UTILITIES.

I inhaled to calm my nerves then turned the worn, brass knob. I heard a thud behind the door, as if something had fallen. Instinct forced me to drop and cover as the small explosive broke the glass, sending it into the hallway. After the grenade exploded, leaving my ears ringing, I looked through the hole where the glass had once been and saw a face staring back at me. I scooted backwards and took a small device from the left pocket of my backpack. I pulled the pin and tossed it through the glassless door. It bounced down the stairs with a metallic *bop, bop, bop.* I heard a *boom* and a scream as the grenade dispatched the guard. I ran down the stairs to find the guard dead in the hallway leading to three other doors—one at the end and one on either side of the small hallway.

The small indicator light on the camera over the farthest door flashed red. I guessed multiple surveillance systems were on the property, and this one was still active. Hoping Abby was behind one of those doors, I picked an order to check them. Starting with the door on the right, I carefully opened it and saw the room was stacked with antique office furniture. There was no space inside for anyone to hide. Two steps across the hallway led me to the second door, which I opened just as carefully. Inside, I found a console, monitors, laptops, and assorted computer gear. The video screens showed several hallways throughout the facility.

As I pulled an explosive device from my pack, someone grabbed me from behind. The grenade drooped to the floor as I fought the attacker. He hit me hard, forcing me toward the console as he grabbed a handful of my hair. He smacked my head into the video screen several times before it broke, spraying blood from my forehead.

He eased his grip as he laughed, maybe thinking he had beaten me. Someone had told me early on to never judge the outcome of a fight until the other man can't get up again. I spun and put the man into an armbar and pushed him into the hallway, not stopping until he smashed against the opposite wall. He still struggled, and I kneed his groin, and he stopped all actions except for grabbing his crotch. When he sat on the floor. I hit him with a hook punch, knocking him out cold.

I rushed back into the room, grabbed the explosive and set the timer to thirty seconds. I exited the room, picked up the downed man, and pushed him inside. I closed the door as I counted. Three, two, one, and then the charge exploded. The hallway camera's light faded—another advantage now in my favor.

Ahead of me was the last door to look behind and the last place in the building Abby could be. Being the only guarded building on the property, she had to be here, and I prayed she will be. Standing in front of the door close enough to smell the dust on the old wood, I took a deep breath and exploded through the door with a push kick just above the antiquated door-knob. The door swung in as I stopped my momentum by grabbing both sides of the door jamb. The door swung open, slammed against the inner wall, and ricocheted to its original position, blocking my view. I squatted and reached to push open the door again. It moved slowly, its hinges emitting a deep, slow squeaking that reminded me of a Halloween fright fest. I was less of a target in this position and had the M16 tight to my shoulder as I looked down its sights. A quick memory of basic training flashed through my mind. *"What's your windage and elevation, Private DeLuca?"* Hell of a time for a memory.

I saw a single dim light over the head of someone— definitely female—tied to a high back chair. I naturally reacted to the situation and went to enter the room.

The gagged figure shook her head in a fashion that indicated, *no, no, no.*

I stopped, realizing the person tied to the chair was my Abby and that she may be hinting at some danger just inside the doorway. My heart ached seeing her in this situation, causing me to want to bolt forward and rescue her. Abby still signaled me not to come closer as I pondered what the problem could be.

I popped a smoke generator capsule I had in my pack, and it revealed an array of laser light beams crisscrossing just beyond the door. I took the pack from my back and removed anything that would fit inside my pockets. Holding the pack in my left hand, I gave it a slight backward swing and tossed it into the beams. A small trap door opened just where I would have been standing if I had gone through the doorway. Abby had just saved my ass; now it was time to return the favor.

I stepped back several paces then ran forward, getting enough momentum to jump across the narrow pit. I landed and checked the room. Seeing no immediate threat, I looked into the pit. Many spiked sticks pointed upward— an old-style trap that would impale the unsuspecting victim, causing a slow death if he was unlucky and an immediate one if he was fortunate.

I approached Abby and she still shook her head. Inspecting the chair, I saw it was sitting on an improvised pressure plate. If I stood her up, the loss of her weight would trigger the explosives tapped to the chair's legs. The improvised devise had two positions—armed and *boom*. With Abby in the chair, the plate had four contact points; wires ran from each point to the explosives. As long as she stayed seated, she would remain alive.

Taine didn't miss a chance to ensure she could eliminate any enemy or any threat. This was proof she didn't care about anything other than her goal, whatever that was. Her desire for revenge and death made me wonder how bad her life had once been and if I would be the same if I had experienced it.

I slung the M16 over my shoulder and stood in front of Abby. I took her face in my hands and kissed her forehead as I untied the gag. With the gag now on the floor, I kissed Abby's lips.

She cried and apologized—for what, I'm not sure. "I thought you were dead, Paolo. They told me you had died in the bank vault. I gave up hope that anyone would look for me. I don't even know what she wants from me."

Abby had a thousand questions and a thousand emotions to accompany them, but this was not the time or place to get into the reasoning behind Taine's actions. I tried to calm her down, but she kept saying, "I don't want to die," repeatedly.

Finally, I yelled as loud as I could, *"Abby! I'm here now!* We can talk about this later, if I can get you out of here."

It stunned her into silence. "What the fuck do you mean *if?* Please get me out of here. Please take me home, Paolo!" She was getting loud again, so I did the only thing I could think of; I gave her a long kiss on her soft quivering lips. Abby calmed down, relaxing just a bit. "Oh, shit."

"Oh shit?" I repeated.

"Yeah, Shit Paolo. You need to help the girl . . . the girl by the door. See if she's okay."

"No need, Abby. She's gone." I already knew she was dead because of the way her body lay across the others underneath her.

Crying hard again, she asked about the girl by the door, the one lying in a heap with the other dead bodies. "I think I know her, Paolo. I saw part of her face before Taine shot her, but it was too dark to see her clearly. Who was she?"

I didn't answer trying to spare Abby from the pain.

"Why aren't you answering me, Paolo?"

Then it hit her like a wrecking ball. Abby knew the girl in the pile, the girl lying at an unnatural angle on top of other dead human beings, was her sibling. I told you she was smart. This time too smart for her own good.

Her tears flowed like a river down the rocky cliff side. I wanted to hug her tight, but because of the chair bomb, I could not. "She was a victim of Taine's bullshit, Abby. I'm sorry I couldn't save her."

"Oh God, Paolo!" Abby exclaimed.

A voice came over what sounded like a fast-food drive-thru speaker. "I told you to stay away from Pennville, Mr. DeLuca, and yet, here you are. Now Miss Woo must die, just as her sister has, and it is your fault that both will be dead, not mine."

Fifteen

Confrontation

Taine's voice triggered something inside me that I had not known in years—a rage not felt since my spotter fell from the helicopter over that dreadful South American jungle. I exploded with a thunderous roar full of emotion.

"Nooooo!" I screamed in the direction of the disembodied voice. "I have what you want, Taine. I brough it here to give to you in exchange for Abby."

No response came from that old Asian bitch. It was quiet in the space, like a mausoleum or crypt. There were no sounds except for Abby's sobbing. I could hear my heart beating and Abby's accelerated breathing heightened her anxiety.

"I have what you want, Taine! The thumb drive full of information, the one your man stole from Franklin Bank.

Seconds passed like centuries.

"The drive you murdered Emma Stone and her children for."

More seconds passed.

"I'll trade it for Abby's life."

Even more time passed.

"Do you hear me, Taine? I'll give you the drive for Abby." And then I did something I had never done before with any enemy I had ever encountered—I begged. "Please . . ."

The wall mounted speaker remained silent as my words hung heavy and unanswered in the air.

"Paolo, what are you talking about?" Abby asked. "What do you have that she could possible want?"

I spoke just loud enough for only Abby to hear. "I have the flash drive her gang stole from the bank when we were there. I took it from one of the crew after I shot him. It has a list of every corrupt politician, police officer, city official, and even the trashmen. You name them, they're on the list. It's our only way out alive, Abby."

Time crawled as nothing came back over the speaker from Taine. I pulled my switchblade from my back pocket and thumbed it open. It set with a *click* as the blade hit the stop. "I'm going to cut you lose, Abby, but I don't want you to move an inch until I say. Do you understand?"

She nodded in affirmation.

I slowly cut the ropes and threw them from the chair. I stood and put my hand on Abby's shoulder.

"What do we do now, Paolo?"

"The only thing we can. We Wait."

Seconds passed like hours as Abby and I waited for whatever would happen. Sometime later, a door at the back of the room opened, and light from the other room infiltrated our semi-darkened space and shone on the pile of bodies just behind Abby. It was part of the crew from the bank and Abby's twin sister.

Abby turned her head just enough to see the way her sister's body lay in a heap on top of the others. Abby turned back and covered her face as she tried to hide her tears—a useless effort.

Taine walked through the door and toward us, but her gait was slow and elderly-like. "Drop your weapon, you'll have no need for it."

I did, and one of her henchmen ran to pick it up.

"Give me the drive, Mr. DeLuca."

"No. We get out first then you get it."

Taine walked within an arm's reach of Abby and pushed her pearl-handled pistol into the back of Abby's head. "Give me what I want, or I will kill her right now."

"No!"

Taine pushed the pistol into the back of Abby's head, forcing her chin to her chest. Taine cocked the hammer. "Give me the drive."

"What the fuck is so important on the drive that you would kill an innocent woman for it?"

"I'm sure you looked at the files on the drive, Mr. DeLuca. If I were you, I would have. As far as your innocent Abby, well, she's a means to an end. Nothing more."

"Please, just release Abby."

"No."

As a last resort, I took the small pistol hidden in my waistband and pointed it at Taine's head." She laughed as four red laser dots appeared on different spots on Abby.

"Motherfuckers!" was all I could think to say as I looked behind me and saw several men pointing automatic weapons at Abby, standing where the hole in the floor used to be.

Back and forth we went, arguing our positions with nothing but Taine's advantage winning out every time. Taine looked at her men, and two more laser dots appeared on the back of Abby's head. Taine lowered her gun, and Abby twisted her head upward, probably to relieve the pain. She sat with her hands grasping the sides of the chair to keep her steady and from falling out of it.

Taine had too much advantage and too many ways of negotiating, all which led to death for the person in question. "Abby's life means nothing to me. I have already killed her twin and her partners from the bank. If you shoot me dead, Mr. DeLuca, the men around you will kill her first, so you can watch her die. And then kill you. Weigh your options carefully. Do you wish to see your girlfriend die in front of you, Mr. DeLuca?" Seconds passed before she spoke again. "Shi Han will put a bullet in her head with no emotion. Well, maybe he will show a smile, as he loves his work. Make your choice, Mr. DeLuca. You only have one."

I looked into Shi Han's eyes and saw his love for his job, but I had another idea to propose. I leveled the gun at Shi Han and fired. The shot killed him instantly.

Taine raised her hand, signaling the others not to retaliate. She spoke with anger. "You are a fool, Mr. DeLuca. This will only end badly for you and Miss Woo. Now give me the drive."

"I will not! Not until Ab..."

Taine raised her weapon and shot me in the left shoulder. The small caliber bullet grazed my skin but still drew blood.

I fell to my knees after staggering backward but still within arms-reach of the woman I loved. Being out of options, I did the only thing I could. I saw the fear in Abby's eyes as I dropped my weapon and outstretched my hand. "Do you trust me, Abby?"

She paused for a moment and then clenched my hand, just like Pitt had earlier today. "Yes."

I nodded and faced Taine. "The only option I have left if you don't let us go is to pull Abby from the chair, setting off the explosives and killing all of us as a result."

Taine was used to getting her way, no matter what, so she again pushed her weapon into the back of Abby's head. "If I kill her now, Mr. DeLuca, she falls forward, and we all die anyway. But she will die before the rest of us do. Most important, you will see her die. What makes you think you have any advantage over me.?" Taine's face showed her anger, turning her gray appearance a shade of crimson.

Taine then walked around the chair, stood in front of Abby and pistol whipped her. The gun drew blood from

Abby's cheek, which dripped to her chin and into her lap. She spoke to Abby in Chinese while looking at me, as If she were translating English into Chinese for Abby's benefit. She was telling Abby to beg me for her life.

Abby replied in a gruff voice which I had never heard before starting in Chinese and the finishing in English. Abby spoke the words slow and deliberate with controlled anger. "You have taken a lot from me, Taine. You took a lifetime of love and friendship from me and my sister. You killed my parents. You controlled my life without me even knowing what you were doing to me. And now you're asking me to beg Paolo for my life." Abby paused as if she were seceding something that would change our lives. She looked me in the eyes with no fear of the future. "Let's do this, Paolo."

I tensed my arm. My bicep expanded the sleeve of my riding gear as I readied to pull Abby from the chair and into my arms, hoping for one last moment in the embrace of the one I loved most in the world. Although it felt like hours, the old woman spoke before I pulled Abby toward me. I thought she could have calculated a reason to disprove Einstein's theory of relativity in those moments between what should have been Abby's last words and my final act of defiance.

"For now, you win Mr. DeLuca." She nodded at the men behind me.

I heard the click of a remote as the red dots disappeared from Abby's head. The lights on the chair charges went off, and it was safe for Abby to stand. She did and then she hugged and kissed me like it would be the last time she ever would.

"Ahh, it's good to see there is still love in this world. Now give me the flash drive so I can be on my way."

"I don't have it on me. It's outside, hidden where only I can find it."

Taine was losing her patience with me. She said something in Chinese and then pulled a knife from her jacket and, in one swift motion, cut Abby across the top of her arm.

Abby screamed as the blood stained the top of her clothes. I placed my hand over her wound, trying to stop the blood flow.

Taine took an irritated breath as she spoke. "You like to live dangerously, Mr. DeLuca. I can kill you both where you stand. You are making this much harder than it needs to be. If you continue to test my generosity, you may regret your decision. I can kill Abby and let you live with the guilt of her death. Her blood will be on your hands, Mr. DeLuca.

"Kill her and you don't get the drive. We both stay alive or you'll never find it without us. I called the police before I came here, and they could be here any minute. If we go now, you'll get the drive and still have time to escape before the cavalry arrives."

Taine looked at the man behind me. He came within arm's reach with his hand held out, palm up. I gave him the

cellphone. The numbers on the phone had no names
attached to them, so he pressed Redial.

Richards answered and said, "Hold on, DeLuca.
We're on our way, should be there in five." The guy
disconnected the call.

Taine had that look again, like her mind was
weighing several scenarios, possibly calculating the time
difference between what she needed to do and how long
before the police arrived. "Kane, lead us out. Keep the
woman in front of us in case a surprise is waiting. Mr.
DeLuca will walk ahead of me."

Abby had a hard time walking after being tied to
that chair. I had told her earlier to be ready to run if we
needed to. She said she would do her best. I slowed some to
let Abby and the guard get far enough ahead so she would
not hear me talking to Taine.

"Answer this, Taine. Why the double for Abby?"

"You wish for a history lesson, Mr. DeLuca? Your
curiosity is admirable in the face of certain difficulty. Your
Abby, as you call her, was the younger of the twin girls
born to the Woos. I managed to get the first born out of the
nursery with no trouble. The nurses took the younger twin,
your Abby, to intensive care because of complications from
the difficult birth. They never told Mrs. Woo the truth
about the twins. At my direction, they told her that the first
girl was still born. I had another family raise her, one loyal
to only me. I see you are not surprised, Mr. DeLuca. You
already know I have contacts in the FBI and other agencies.
I knew Mrs. Woo despised living in Texas. Who do you

think placed the idea of moving to Philadelphia in her head?”

“Who’s your man inside the marshal service?”

“I thought that would be plain to you by now, Mr. DeLuca. I intended only to use the girls to lure the Woo’s back to China as a diplomatic ploy, one that would win me favor with the other branches of the triad; a favor that would give me access to direct dealings in China. But then, things went wrong. The car accident was not supposed to kill the Woos, just give us time to take the second child from them. Fortunately for her, the car seat saved her life; however, her parents were not as lucky. Do you know the saying, *The best laid plans,* Mr. DeLuca?

“I’ve heard it before.”

“Well then, let me finish with this. Your Abby was to be, as you say, the fall guy for the bank robbery. Since she was always going into the bank vault, it was an opportunity to get what I needed.”

“The thumb drive I presume.”

“Yes, the thumb drive. An unfortunate mistake on my part. Once again, I trusted a man. And that trust caused all of this, and, as a result of his insubordination, he was hanged in Franklin Park. Abby knew the bank manager, called her by her first name. The police would think the two had planned the robbery. Abby would be the mastermind, and the manager would be a disgruntled employee. I would then kill my accomplices in the robbery to hide any trace to me. No matter if any of them lived or died, either way, I would have the drive. But I did make one mistake. I did not count on one variable, Mr. DeLuca. You."

"But the safety deposit box was leased to Computer Logic. Isn't that one of your companies?"

"Yes' However, Fu Lao thought he could extort money from me to get my property back. As your gender so often does, Mr. DeLuca, he thought he was superior to any female. That was his mistake and ultimately got him killed. Since I could not get the device through any of my contacts, I had to use your Miss Woo and the bank manager to get what I wanted. So now you see I mean exactly as I say, Mr. DeLuca—no man will ever get anything from me by force, ever again. If I need to end someone's life, I will—including yours."

We had reached the top of the stairs and headed down the main hallway to the front doors. I filled in some blanks, so Taine did not have to keep talking about her empire. "Your accountant attempted to lease the box from Franklin Bank without your knowledge, then he downloaded the information onto the drive, wiped the server and put the only copy inside the deposit box. I bet he was threating to give it to the government if you didn't pay out. I'm betting he threatened to release all the info to the press, unless you made him a rich man."

"Yes."

"Then you found a way around him, and that involved Abby, her sister, and the bank manager."

She nodded. "Now, Mr. DeLuca, before I let you and Abby go, perhaps to die another day, give me the flash drive."

"Abby and I get on the bike first. When we get to the gate, I'll leave the drive on the ground, and we'll call it even."

"No! I want the drive now. I am finished being generous with your lives, Mr. DeLuca."

Everyone around us raised their weapons at Abby and me. The sound of sirens broke the silence of the afternoon.

"Here comes the cavalry!" I emphasized the noise with a nod of my head, even though I didn't have to.

Taine pulled the switchblade and triggered the blade. She grabbed Abby's shirt collar and kicked her behind the knee, forcing Abby to the ground—an agile move for an old woman. Pulling back Abby's hair Taine put the knife to Abby's throat. "I am tired of this game, Mr. DeLuca. Give me the drive, or I will slice the throat of your princess."

Abby looked up at Taine. "Fuck you, bitch! Don't give it to her, Paolo. I'm sick of her shit!" Abby pulled Taine's wrist in a feeble attempt to distance the knife from her throat.

As the first police cruisers came into view, Taine signaled her men. They huddled around her as she gave more orders in Chinese. She released Abby while her henchmen pointed their weapons at us, still guarding the matriarch in case I tried anything. Abby got off the ground and stood behind me, almost hiding from Taine, as a child would hide from a monster behind a parent.

Taine raised her hand, and an Identical pearl-colored escalade to the one I had immobilized earlier careened behind her and her men. Seconds later, another escalade pulled up behind it just as the full contingent of law moved into position, blocking any escape from the compound. At least a hundred weapons now pointed at Taine and her men. The only problem was Abby and I stood between the two, armed groups; it was not a good place for us to be. It was a standoff that any movie plot would be proud of—she can't kill Abby and me, and the law can't kill Taine and her men without killing us. I saw only one way to end this cluster fuck of a day.

I looked at Taine, "The drive is in the taillight of the bike."

Taine nodded at one of her henchmen. He approached the bike and busted the taillight with the butt of his weapon. The drive hit the ground, and he picked it up and held it in the air for Taine to see. Taine silently signaled her men, and they moved as a group, still protecting her.

The doors of the escalade opened, and they lifted Taine into the vehicle, then the first vehicle in line filled with the remainder of her men. The vehicles drove off, but, after just a few seconds, one stopped. The right rear window opened, and Taine tossed a package onto the ground in front of Abby. Before the window closed, the vehicle was moving again, following the other around the side of the main building.

Abby picked it up and opened its cover. The box contained an FBI evidence envelope with all the items that had been in her safety deposit box, including her necklace. It also held one more item—a necklace almost identical to Abby's. The only difference between the two was the diamond; this one was a deep pink color. Abby held the two necklaces in her hand, and I held Abby as she cried again for the loss of a sister she never knew. By giving Abby the envelope, Taine was still telling us she could reach anyone she wanted to. After all, here was a large manila envelope labeled *FBI* with the word *Evidence* in red underneath the initials.

As the law enforcement agents approached, Brennan was the first to arrive. "Damn, Paolo, I missed all the fun! Are you guys okay?"

"We need the medics. We're both hurt."

"You were shot, DeLuca."

"It's barely a scratch but still hurts like hell."

Brennan kissed me on the cheek, her hand lingered a bit too long on my shoulder. "Thank God you're not dead."

Abby hit Brennan in the jaw with a right hook, sending Brennan to the ground as blood spouted from her mouth. "Stay the fuck away from him, *bitch*!"

I guess she had enough of the other-woman thing for one day. Diego helped Brennan up as he tried to contain a smile. Brennan bent over to collect a tooth from the ground.

Two FBI guys and some of the locals were laughing and commenting on the incident. Brennan shot them a nasty sneer, and then she and Diego headed for their car. Diego tried to get her to an EMT, but she yanked her arm from his grip, stormed to the car and slammed the door after getting inside.

"Who the *fuck* was that, Paolo?"

"She helped me find you."

"Do you want that bitch?"

"I came here for you, Abby, no one else."

"Can you take me home, please?"

I put my arms around her and whispered, "Yeah. As soon as medical checks us out, I'll get us a ride."

Sixteen

Aftermath

The feds—and by that, I mean several different branches of government law enforcement, like the FBI, the US Marshals, the DEA, the ATF, Army CID, and any alphabetic and numeric combination agency—all had a contingent of agents going in and out of every building in the compound. It looked like a Fourth of July parade, minus the marching band of course. They found what I expected they would—drugs, money of many currencies, weapons caches supposedly stolen from the military, electronics of every size, and most importantly, thirty women of different cultures used as sex slaves.

Richards asked if we were okay. After I answered in the affirmative, he told me he had emailed a copy of the information on the drive to every news outlet in the city. It was evident word had gotten out, because every news van, every reporter, and every wannabe news caster clamored behind the yellow police-line tape.

"Take a look around, DeLuca, this is all your doing. Can you guess who's not here?"

Several members of the law who should be here but were not, told me what Richards was saying was true. Lee was nowhere to be found, and McGregor sat on the steps to the main building, looking as if he had lost his best friend. A career in law enforcement hadn't showed him that a wolf in sheep's clothing had indeed lived among him and his fellow FBI agents. This would be the sad end to his career because he would be the scapegoat for the FBI. It would go something like, *"If the agent who worked with Lee every day did not have a suspicion of his partner's involvement with known criminals, and if he did know and did not report those suspicions to his superiors, then the Bureau has no choice but to relieve Agent McGregor of his duties."*

The news vans lined the perimeter of the property and filmed everything that moved. They had followed the caravan of emergency vehicles to Pennville just hoping to run that breaking-news ticker along the bottom of the screen.

Richards told us he had called a friend at Channel Three and briefed him on what was about to transpire. He told his friend to call everyone he knew because there would be enough news to go around, and it appears he did just that.

The reporters shouted questions to no one in particular, and even if they heard them, no one dared answer. The FBI finally had had enough and sent a representative for all the agencies to the main gate. He told them, as a group, that if they continued to disrupt the investigation, he would detain each and every one of them, along with and among the suspects currently in custody. It did nothing to persuade them from shouting questions or begging for answers. The only thing this did was to force the news outlets to report the story without knowing the truth, kind of like they always do anyway.

Soon the reporters were distracted from the crime scene when the political elite arrived and got their political faces on camera to condemn any politician or officer involved with Taine and her organization. The governor strode around with his arms flailing, walking behind his contingent of state police security team.

"What a fucking circus!" Richards said as he told Abby and me, he would get us home.

Some high-level director approached us and just started bitching about this and that. "We have a goddamn high body count in there, Mr. DeLuca. How many of them belong to you?"

I pled ignorance, after which Richards intervened. "None." He told the director he had taken out the guards in the attic, at the front door, and then at the front entrance. "Are you sure you want to go with that story, Richards? It takes some serious skill to make those shots from that distance. If you're lying, it could mean your shield."

"Yeah, it's like I said, attic, door, and gate, in that order. One round, one kill—just like they taught us in ranger training. I was special forces, Mr. Director, and I don't appreciate you doubting my word. Now write this down, so I don't have to repeat myself. I arrived here before the rest of you clowns and saw Taine's crew trying to kill Mr. DeLuca. I stepped up and dispatched anything I thought was a threat to him."

"What about the rest of the bodies inside, Detective Richards? A lot of blown-up shit is down in that basement, and I don't see any reason for you to have taken any actions like that."

"Don't you think Taine would do that to cover her tracks and any evidence of her ties to this facility? For God's sake, I don't fucking understand how some of you guys get a government job. I'd like to see the entrance exam for the FBI." Finally, the director gave up and walked away.

Richards smiled, "That man really has a stick up his ass."

The feds and the locals debated who had jurisdiction on the case against Taine. Richards heard the municipal cops and the state police pulled over three pearl-colored escalades and Taine wasn't in any of them. My guess was that she never left the grounds; she's probably in hiding in another subbasement of one of the buildings. I couldn't put anything past her—she had money, the means, and people on the inside. It could be an FBI guy, like Lee, who helped Taine escape today; I had money on guys like Lee—that tiny little Asian bitch with a Napoleon complex. But that would be profiling, and I tried my best never to judge anyone by the color of their skin.

Richards had confiscated my weapons and placed them in the trunk of his cruiser. He took Abby and I into custody and drove us to Philly. The radio was on, but the audio was down and competing for space with the police radio.

"Hey, Richards. Turn that up, will you?" I told him more than asked him.

"I'm Anita Ross with the WPNN On the Nines News," the news reader said to open the two-minute broadcast. "An unknown source has supplied crucial information that has the potential to take down the Chinese crime syndicate known as the triad. The information contained within the file also accuses several high-level police officials, FBI, and political members of money laundering and bribery. This information appears to be tied into the events currently unfolding at the Pennville State School and Hospital facility in Spring City, Pennsylvania, and may be tied to the robbery of the Franklin Bank and Trust less than two weeks ago."

Richards turned off the radio. "Enough of that shit. Someone left a flash drive on my desk, and, when I opened it, I saw all this information—names, places, amounts of money paid out. I had the rook make copies and hand deliver them to all the news outlets in the city. I'm not sure who left it there, but I figured they wanted it to go public."

"Thank God for good Samaritans!"

Abby spoke for the first time since we left Pennville. "I hope they fry that Taine bitch when they find her."

On the ride to Philly, Richards and I discussed the events that had unfolded at Pennville as Abby slept with her head on my shoulder. We collaborated our stories to a detail that those in authority would believe—well, more acceptable than believable. Richards would take responsibility for the kills, but he could say they were necessary for the protection of two kidnapped victims of the Franklin Bank robbery and that it was his duty to do so as a sworn officer of the law.

Richards said, "Your gut was right, DeLuca."

"Yeah, it was. I knew Lee had to be involved with Taine. He acted like he was above it all. I didn't see him at the asylum, but I'm sure he was there. I know his partner was."

Richards smiled as he spoke. "Diego said McGregor told him that Lee had been reassigned before all this went down. But it's like I said to you and Blondie at my office, smells like shit to me."

Abby sat up, spoke up, and sneered at me at the mere mention of Brennan. "If that Blondie is that cop bitch, don't mention her again, or the way I'm feeling today, I'll punch you in your fucking head, Paolo!"

Richards chortled. "I see why you love her so much, bro. She has no problem speaking her mind!"

Abby almost cracked a smile.

The topic of Brennan's involvement in Abby's rescue will go unmentioned for now; there would be time for that later. I'm sure it would take a few days of arguing and then the silent treatment and some nights sleeping on the couch, but it is all worth it to have Abby back. If Brennan was to be a thorn in the side of our relationship, then I'll learn to live with it, if Abby wants not to discuss her involvement.

Richards pulled into Abby's driveway and put the car in park. Shutting off the ignition, he turned and looked over the back seat. "I'll make sure you get your gear back, DeLuca. I know a man gets attached to things, so, after a few days in the evidence locker, I'll sign out the weapons and bring them to you when all this shit settles down.

"Thanks, Richards. I'd hate to lose any of them. We've been together for a long time. Are you sure you're up for the scrutiny?"

He smiled again. "No problem. Kirkman once told me about this lieutenant who saved his ass on an op in Panama. I'm just returning the favor."

I reached over the seat and shook his hand. This bond of brotherhood, forged in common interest, was something members of the military enjoyed, even if they didn't serve together.

Abby and I exited the cruiser. She paused and asked Richards to get out of the car. He did, and Abby grasped him in a hug that even longtime friends rarely received. She thanked him for helping me save her, and, before we went inside, she kissed him softly on his two-day bearded cheek. He smiled at us as he backed out of the driveway.

The Rubins were already at Abby's house, and, when we got inside, they were all hugs and kisses and tears for a joyous reunion. Abby hugged her mother for quite a while then stood in front of her father with her head down. She apologized for yelling at him the last time we had been together.

Trying to bolster a firm appearance, he said, "It's good that you're sorry." His words hung there for a moment, and Abby looked puzzled. "Now tell me you forgive me for being a stubborn, overprotective father."

Abby jumped into his arms and kissed his cheek several times. "I love you, Daddy!" Tears started all over again.

The four of us sat together as Abby and I recounted the story of the past few days. The Rubins, although silent, looked at me quizzingly and sometimes in amazement as Abby told them what happened in the basement room and how I fought to get her back.

"And here we thought you were just a mechanic, Paolo," Mrs. Rubin said.

I smiled as Mr. Rubin placed his hand on my left shoulder—a gesture of acceptance and gratitude.

Abby cried again as she told her parents the details about her sister and how she wished she knew her before all of this happened. Mrs. Rubin had her hands over top of Abby's which rested on the table. Mrs. Rubin said that if it was meant to be, the Creator would have seen to it, and if they had known Abby had a twin sister, they would have adopted both girls. Then she eyed her husband and tilted her head in my direction. Mr. Rubin looked back at her and said something in Yiddish.

He finally looked in my direction at his wife's urging. "Mr. DeLuca, I am not good at times like these, but I must also ask you for your forgiveness. I may have . . . overreacted when we saw you at the hospital. It's just that we could not bear children of our own, because we believe the Creator wanted to bring Abby here to live with us. I pray you can find it in your heart to accept my apologies.

Sometimes my mouth starts talking before my brain knows what it wants to say."

I told the Rubins there was nothing to forgive them for. They had not wronged me with their concerns for the safety of their daughter or their Creator's plan for them as a couple. I also told them that I wish I had known that kind of love when I was growing up.

Mr. Rubin stood and extended his hand. I stood and accepted it as a show of respect for him as a man and a father, and then he unexpectedly hugged me.

"I should have trusted my Abby's judgement."

"Thank you," I said. "Mr. Rubin, I believe only one God exists, and she, in all her greatness, had challenged man with different beliefs, to one day they may have a discussion that would lead to an understanding for all faiths. And I prayed that one day, man in general, would finally stop the bullshit fighting over an idea that they were the only true believers in God and that everyone else is wrong."

Mr. Rubin huffed. "Maybe you were a holy man in a previous life, Paolo. You seem wise beyond your years."

We sat again and I sipped my coffee. "Mrs. Rubin, may I ask you what you called Marshal Brennan at the hospital?"

"You can ask."

Mr. Rubin look at his wife and then at me. "My lovely wife, who is normally not so judgmental, called your friend a *sharilila.* It more or less translates to *slut.*"

Abby laughed as Mrs. Rubin defended herself. "What? A woman knows these things!"

Abby and I cleaned the dishes after the Rubins left then went to bed. Sleeping next to Abby again felt like coming home. I was more than happy she was where she belonged.

I was up the next morning about an hour before Abby. I sat outside in the shade of the screened porch, drinking black coffee and reading the paper. Headlines about the Pennville affair were followed by photos of Taine, and many others graced the front page. Names were revealed, and the article said the numerous investigations would begin into those named in the file.

Abby came out and kissed me good morning. She sat with her black coffee in her favorite mug and placed the box Taine had tossed at her onto the bistro table. After sipping her coffee, she took both necklaces from the box and held them in her fists, as if she were channeling a lost soul. She put them on and looked so beautiful with her sister's necklace complimenting her own. Abby smiled at some unknown thoughts, hopefully about her sister being in a better place. She organized the pile of papers and opened the parchment detailing her family tree.

In the lower left-hand corner, Taine had written several Chinese characters, and then in English wrote, *all this is truth, Taine.* Abby traced her hand over them as tears welled up again.

"What do they mean Abby?"

"They say that my name has always been Abhijishya Woo, and that with the death of my sister, Abhijaya, I am only one of a few remaining descendants of the Ming Dynasty who can prove her claim of royal bloodlines back to the emperor." Abby picked up the handwritten note next to the new writings and read it. "It's from Taine. She says that if I ever reveal any of this information or act upon it to try to claim my birthright, she will kill both of us without so much as a second thought. She also said that's what my sister planned to do, and that's why she killed her." Abby choked up, saying she could not understand how Taine could be so giving and so cruel all in the same day.

I told her that, as with the rest of the world, it was all about control by someone with only two goals in life— one was to rule and the other was to control the wealth. I added that those were the reasons for the world being as screwed up as it was.

"Listen, Paolo. I know I made you promise that you would never do what you did to save me but thank you for breaking that promise. I love you!"

"I broke that promise because I could not lose you, Abby." I stifled a sob. "Without you . . ." I paused again, trying not to cry. "I have nothing."

Abby smiled and got out of her chair. She sat on my lap and kissed me deeply. She repeated, "I love you," several times. We stayed like that for a long time, not saying a word, just enjoying the moment. Abby wiped the tears from her eyes. "Let's go to Verdi's for dinner tonight."

"Are you sure? It's been a rough couple of days."

"I feel like celebrating. I'll give them a call, make a reservation. And with that, she was off to get her cell.

"Wait! What about your performance tonight? I thought you were thinking about going. You said you needed it."

"All I need is you, Paolo."

When Abby returned, she told me we had a reservation for eight, and that her parents were coming, and that I needed to invite Detective Richards.

I smiled at her. "One more thing, Abby. How come you never told me you spoke Chinese?"

"How come you never asked?"

Seventeen

Texas

Abby and I didn't talk much about all the things that happened at Franklin Bank or at Pennville, not since the night we told her parents everything that had transpired. Abby also decided to attend the performance at the Kimmel Center. When she was introduced, the audience stood and applauded for a full two minutes. Her single tear of joy overshadowed the still-visible sadness and the bruise on her cheek. She spoke two words—"Thank you"—then had the best performance of the night.

We celebrated Abby's return at Verti Restorante with some of her friends from the Philharmonic, her parents, and Richards. The dinner conversation remained lighthearted, and the food proved to delicious to describe with only words. I sat between Abby and her father. We talked about my career in the army, I told him more about those years of my life than I have told Abby. He shook his head often in agreement and sometimes in disgust at what I told him about Iran, Iraq, Afghanistan, and about MoJo.

"My mother was very young when the allies liberated Auschwitz, almost a baby," he said, wiping a tear. "I am still amazed that after all the stories of horror the survivors of the camps have told that this world is still in such bad shape. History repeats itself, Paolo, no matter what we say or do. Maybe the Creator will someday stop all the madness."

I raised my glass of wine and looked him in the eyes. "To the Creator . . ."

"Shalom!"

Mrs. Rubin, who was sitting to my left, spoke up after Mr. Rubin's blessing of peace over our meal. "Paolo, Abby says you have good news."

"Yes. Well, sort of. My mother actually called. She said she saw the news and wanted to check in."

"Well . . . when will we meet her? I can't wait to talk to another mother."

I told her my mother always says she will come, and then, at the last minute she'll back out. "It's always been that way, Mrs. Rubin. She'll never win the Mother of the Year award."

"Well . . . you'll always have me, Paolo!"

To which I responded, "*L'Chayim*!" Which everyone laughed at. "To Life!" we all shouted.

*****

That following morning, things got a little heated, because I mentioned Brennan again. To me, Brennan was a kindred spirit, a friend, someone of importance to me, maybe from a past life or some mystical bullshit like that, I don't know. In respect to that spirit, I wanted Abby to understand the connection I had with Brennan. It's not like I wanted to have her around all the time; I just wanted Abby to respect the friendship. They didn't need to be close friends or anything else. But Abby still had this insecurity about our relationship even though I have told her repeatedly that she was the only woman I loved. I know it has to do with her birthparents and her abandonment issues, but I will never leave Abby alone in this world, and she needs to realize that.

Abby kept playing me off. "I need my coffee first, Paolo."

I pushed a little more, trying to get the conversation flowing, but she would have none of it.

"Abby, we need to talk about this Brennan thing sooner or later. I'd like it to be sooner and get it out of the way."

"No . . . We don't!" she said with a long pause between *no* and the *we don't"* She emphasized the *no* slowly with her eyebrows raised and her head slightly to the right. That was Abby's way of telling me that no really meant no and that I should stop talking, if I knew what was good for me.

"Yes, Abby, we do. And we need to do it now."

"If you want that bitch so bad, go to her and don't come back, Paolo!"

"Abby, I don't want her! I want to find out what happened the last time we talked. The way she was talking to me was like she thought I was someone else. I need to know why. I want you to come to Texas with me to talk with her. It may be easier for her to open up about what happened if you are there too."

"I fucking said *no,* Paolo. I don't want to go to Texas. I don't want to talk to her, especially about you.

Right now, I don't even want to talk to you about you!"
Abby punctuated every statement with the bang of a spoon
against her coffee cup as she stirred half-and-half into the
mix. She stirred so hard that the cup broke in two and
spilled onto the countertop and the floor. *This is bullshit,
Paolo!"*

"Abby, please stop yelling! I'm asking you to do
this one thing for me. God, how I hate having to say this to
you, but how many times did I go to the bank with you?
How many drunken nights did we talk for hours about your
birth parents? How many internet searches did I do for
you? I'm not asking you this as a form of repayment. I'm
asking you to do this one thing for me!"

"Why is this so damn important to you, Paolo? You
don't owe her anything."

"I kind of do owe her. She helped me find you. I
just need to know, Abby—like you did about your
birthparents."

Abby sighed in defeat as she cleaned the coffee
from the counter and floor. "Okay, Paolo. I'll do this for
you, this one time, but I will talk to her alone! *You will not
talk to Brennan!* Do you understand me?"

Abby had never given me an order before. It was
the first and hopefully the last in our relationship. I quietly
said, "Okay, we'll do it your way."

"You're God damn right we'll do it my way. I'm
doing this for you, Paolo. I'm not doing anything for that
woman, other than talking to her—no favors, no hugs, and

certainly not the girlfriend thing, but mostly because you always stuck by me without question. And because I love you."

I remained silent as I launched the contacts list on my cell. I thumbed Brennan's name and hit Send. Surprisingly, she answered on the third ring. I told her that Abby and I were coming to Texas to see her. She didn't put up much of an argument about it; although she said she really didn't want to see me. She made the last part very clear.

"I understand you don't want to see me, Brennan, but we're coming anyway."

"Abby is coming too?"

"Yeah, that's the agreement. She wants to talk with you. Alone."

The phone was silent.

I asked her for her condo's address, and she gave it to me with a reluctant voice. Then she disconnected without a word.

*****

We caught a flight to Dallas/Fort Worth, and, upon arrival, we went straight to the airport express hotel. I signed for the room as Abby paid the cabby, who gave the bags to the bellman. Abby and I barely spoke on the plane because I didn't want to start anything we couldn't walk away from. It was the longest flight I had ever been on but not in actual time, only in quiet.

We ate dinner in the room that night, and, since it was so quiet, I put on the news to see what was happening. The local news was about two US Marshals receiving distinguished service awards for their assistance in the takedown of a major crime syndicate operating on the east coast and for their help in the rescue of two civilians who had been kidnapped during a bank robbery. While the newsreader reported the story, Diego's and Brennan's photos appeared on the screen.

"I just can't get away from this shit, even halfway across the country!"

I glanced at her, not sure how to respond. "Sure seems that way, don't it?"

Abby shot me that look again. "You're such an ass!"

*****

We entered the lobby of the Sycamore high rise at ten thirty the following morning after the security guard buzzed the door. "Good morning, Miss Woo," he said. "Ms. Brennan said for you to go right up and for Mr. DeLuca to wait here."

Abby went straight to the elevator without missing a step; it was as if someone had programmed the lift to open as soon as she was within three feet of the door. When she turned around as the doors closed, I couldn't tell if she was looking at me or not. Those white rimmed sunglasses hid her emotions well.

When the doors closed, the guard instructed me to have a seat. "You might want to get comfortable, Mr. DeLuca. You might be here a while."

I guess he knew something I didn't.

Heading to the couch, I snatched a complimentary copy of the *Dallas Morning Star*, and, like any man, I turned to the sports page. It was getting close to football season, and I read all of the sports section then the rest of the paper from cover to cover. I also flipped through several magazines and was just closing the cover on the latest issue of *House and Garden* when the guard buzzed in someone.

A man wearing a shirt that read *Juan's Tex-Mex Grill* greeted the guard like they were old friends. *"Que pasa, mi amigo?"*

To which the guard responded, *"Nada mucho.* How many times this week? Six?"

The delivery guy responded, "More like ten. She must really be on a bender this time." He was in the elevator and back down within a matter of minutes. He approached me and asked, "Are you DeLuca?"

"Yeah . . .why?"

"This smoking hot babe named Abby told me to tell you to go to lunch and come back for her at four. She said you would cover the bill and the tip."

I gave him a twenty.

He looked at it and the at me. "What about the delivery charge?"

"I just gave you twenty for the food!"

"*Nooo,* for the message delivery, *amigo!*"

I gave him another ten and told him to go.

He left with the standard, *"Hasta la vista,"* and then, *"Adios, gringo!"*

Under my sarcastic breath, I told him, "Yeah, go fuck yourself, *perra.*"

Once he was gone the guard told me about a place that was within walking distance that had great food and that it would be better than sitting here for the next four hours. I agreed and headed outside into the warm afternoon sun.

Several blocks away, I found the place, of course it was called Texas's Best Bar-B-Q. It was the second best I ever had. After two sandwiches and several beers, I returned to Brennan's condo.

After the guard buzzed me into the lobby, the elevator doors opened, and Abby exited just like she had walked in—not missing a stride. She spoke loudly as she passed me, "Let's go home, stud."

"What . . .? Wait . . .! What . . .?"

The guard laughed. "Better run along now, like a good little boy!"

As we headed outside, I asked Abby what had happened with Brennan.

"We talked girl talk."

"Yeah? And . . .?"

And that's it."

"That's it? What do you mean, *that's it?*"

Abby smiled. "What don't you understand about *that's it?*"

"Aren't you going to tell me what she said?"

"Nope!"

"Nothing?"

"Honestly, I don't understand why men are so clueless."

Following Abby through the lobby to the door—and always being the gentleman—I held the door for her, as she had grown accustomed to.

She smiled at this simple romantic gesture. "Thanks, love."

As Abby went through, a gorgeous redheaded woman in a short, tight white dress entered. I held the door for her too.

Admiring her beauty, and her flaming-red hair exploding with curls, I hoped Abby didn't notice me looking just a bit too long. "You're welcome."

Speaking those last two words as I turned to follow Abby outside, I glimpsed a tattoo appearing just below the waistline on the woman's exposed back. It was so familiar, yet I didn't place it. Those few seconds gnawed at the recesses of my mind. My intuition told me something was odd, but it never pulled the trigger on the idea something was about to happen. Instead of lingering, I let go of the glass door, ready to follow Abby to the airport limo. The woman headed for the reception desk and announced in stride that she was here to see Marshal Brennan. Her words slipped through the crack of the closing door as Abby called out to me, "Are you coming, Paolo?"

I heard Abby, but I also heard the young woman. "Yeah, right behind you, babe." Without another thought, I watched the door close behind me.

As we rode to the hotel in frustrating silence, Abby looked at me and took pity on me. "Okay, I'll tell you just this. She said you remind her of her father."

Philadelphia

Arriving home late, Abby and I were exhausted but too tired to sleep. Showering and now ready to relax, I stood by the couch just outside the sliding glass doors leading to Abby's Asian-inspired patio—a place where we loved being together.

The small television hidden in plain view in the veranda's corner flickered to life, and I adjusted the volume to almost a whisper. Late night advertisements for fast food and medications filled the airwaves with promises of fulfillment of hunger and lust. I stood sipping chamomile tea—a remedy Abby taught me was also good for helping get to sleep.

I watched as the news broadcast began with a flash of their Breaking News banner scrolling across the screen. The reporter spoke words that stabbed at my heart. I listened in disbelief as the reporter repeated the narration.

"Once again, breaking news out of Dallas Texas. A night time security guard found United States Marshal Jane Brennan brutally murdered in her upscale midtown apartment. Brennan was instrumental in the recent takedown of the Chines Triad operating out of Philadelphia. Investigators have not named any persons of interest in her murder; however, members of the marshal's service and the FBI speaking off the record believe her death was retribution for her part in the dismantling of the crime syndicate. We'll have more on this story . . ."

Abby came walking out of the house and stood beside me. "hey, Paolo. What do you think of moving the .

. .” and then she stop talking as she saw the look upon my face and the wetness in my eyes, “What’s wrong, Paolo?”

I couldn’t speak, so I just pointed to the monitor with the remote still in my hand. She watched as the newsreader reported the day’s events again, this time from the Texas affiliate.

“Oh my God, Paolo! I am so sorry.” Then she put her arms around me as I cried silently at the loss of another comrade.